Man From Nowhere

Spock was stepping through the door when the voice spoke. "You came! Thank God! There's still time!"

Everyone whirled, phasers out. Kirk looked up. On the cliff above them stood a man. He wore a ripped and disheveled jumper suit. He was a big man, but his face had been badly battered. A dark bruise had swollen his jaw. "It's not too late!" he cried down to them. "We can still stop him!" He extended his hands in appeal. "But I . . . I need your help . . . please . . . help me . . ."

He reeled, clutching at his throat. Then his knees buckled —and he tumbled, headlong, from the cliff.

Kirk and Spock ran to him. His body lay unmoving, but massive physical power was still latent in it. Who was he? What were he and his spacecraft doing on this "routine" planet?

STAR TREK 10

BANTAM PATHFINDER EDITIONS

A comprehensive and fully integrated series designed to meet the expanding needs of the young adult reading audience and the growing demand among readers of all ages for paperback books of high quality.

Bantam Pathfinder Editions provide the best in fiction and nonfiction in a wide variety of subject areas. They include novels by classic and contemporary writers; vivid, accurate histories and biographies; authoritative works in the sciences; collections of short stories, plays and poetry.

Bantam Pathfinder Editions are carefully selected and approved. They are presented in a new and handsome format, durably bound and printed on specially selected high-quality paper.

Bantam Books by James Blish
Ask your bookseller for the books you have missed

SPOCK MUST DIE!
STAR TREK
STAR TREK 2
STAR TREK 3
STAR TREK 4
STAR TREK 5
STAR TREK 6
STAR TREK 7
STAR TREK 8
STAR TREK 9
STAR TREK 10

STAR TREK 10
JAMES BLISH

Based on the Exciting
Television Series Created by
GENE RODDENBERRY

BANTAM PATHFINDER EDITIONS
TORONTO / NEW YORK / LONDON

RLI: VLM 8 (VLR 7–11) / IL 6–adult

STAR TREK 10
A Bantam Book / published February 1974
2nd printing
3rd printing

All rights reserved.
Copyright © 1974 by Bantam Books, Inc. and
Paramount Pictures Corporation.
This book may not be reproduced in whole or in part, by
mimeograph or any other means, without permission.
For information address: Bantam Books, Inc.

Published simultaneously in the United States and Canada

Bantam Books are published by Bantam Books, Inc. Its trademark, consisting of the words "Bantam Books" and the portrayal of a bantam, is registered in the United States Patent Office and in other countries. Marca Registrada. Bantam Books, Inc., 666 Fifth Avenue, New York, New York 10019.

PRINTED IN THE UNITED STATES OF AMERICA

to KARIN
who also wanted to set Spock to music

Contents

Preface	ix
THE ALTERNATIVE FACTOR	1
THE EMPATH	27
THE GALILEO SEVEN	53
IS THERE IN TRUTH NO BEAUTY?	82
A PRIVATE LITTLE WAR	109
THE OMEGA GLORY	137

PREFACE

You've given me a surprise. I put no prefaces to *Star Trek* 7 and 8, simply because I had no news to report, no questions I hadn't answered before, and nothing that I felt needed further explanation. As the mail response to those books came in, I found quite a few of you asking to have the prefaces back, because they contributed an added "personal touch." I didn't have those letters when I wrote the preface to *Star Trek* 9, where in fact I did simply have a few new things to say. Up to that point, I'd regarded my role as nothing but that of a pipeline between the scripts and all the rest of you who can't forget the series. After all, neither the main concept of Star Trek nor a single one of its episodes came from me —instead, I was doing the equivalent of transposing some works of other composers to a different key, or at best making a piano version of works originally written for orchestra. I've written other books which were—and are —wholly mine, and where I haven't hesitated to inflict my own feelings on the readers, but in this series it was obviously my duty to the originals to keep myself *out* of them as much as possible.

Well, I really have nothing to report again this time, but I do want to thank you for asking me to go back to peeking around the corner, as it were. I'm still keeping myself out of the Star Trek stories as much as I can—in fact, more and more as I've gained practice at it—but it is nice to know that you also like my cameo bits at the front. Vanity is one of the main drives of every author except the greatest, as I've seen not only in myself but in the fifty or more I've talked to and/or had as friends over more decades than I care to count. For those of you who want more than a peek back, and in answer to another question which pops up often in your letters, there are those other books, a couple of dozen, which you could find rather easily; they're almost all still in print. That's an order, Mr. Spock.

James Blish
July, 1973

THE ALTERNATIVE FACTOR

(Don Ingalls)

The planet offered such routine readings to the *Enterprise* sensors that Kirk ordered a course laid in for the nearest Star Base. "We can be on our way," he was telling the helmsman when Spock lifted his head from his computer. He said, "Captain, there is—"

He never completed his sentence. The *Enterprise* heaved in a gigantic lurch. A deafening grinding sound hammered at its hull—and the ship went transparent. From where he'd been flung, Kirk could see the stars shining through it. Then static crashed insanely as though the universe itself were wrenching in torment. Abruptly, stillness came. The ship steadied. The vast convulsion was over.

Bruised people, sprawled on the deck, began to edge cautiously back to their bridge stations. Kirk hauled himself back to his feet. "What in the name of— Mr. Spock!"

Spock was already back at his computer. "Captain, this is incredible! I read—"

Again the mighty paroxysm interrupted him. There came the ship's headlong plunge, the grinding roar, its appalling transparency. Kirk struggled once more to his feet and ran, ashen-faced, to Spock's station. "What is it?" he shouted.

"What my readings say is totally unbelievable, sir. Twice—for a split second each time—everything within range of our instruments seemed on the verge of winking out!"

Still shaken, Kirk said, "Mr. Spock! I want facts! Not poetry!"

"I have given you facts, Captain. The entire magnetic field in this solar system simply blinked. That planet below us, whose mass I was measuring, attained zero gravity."

Kirk stared at him. "But that's impossible! What you are describing is . . . why, it's—"

"Nonexistence, Captain," Spock said.

Mingled horror and awe chilled Kirk. He heard Uhura speak. "There's a standard general-alert signal from Star Fleet Command, Captain!"

He raced for his mike. "This is the Captain speaking. All stations to immediate alert status. Stand by . . ."

Spock looked over at him. "Scanners now report a life object on the planet surface, sir."

"But only five minutes ago you made a complete life survey of it! What's changed?"

"This life reading only began to appear at approximately the same moment that the shock phenomena subsided."

And this was the routine planet that concealed no surprises! Kirk drew a deep breath. "What is its physical make-up?"

"A living being. Body temperature, 98.1 Fahrenheit. Mass . . . electrical impulses . . . it is apparently human, Captain."

"And its appearance coincided with your cosmic 'wink-out'?"

"Almost to the second."

"Explanation?"

"None, Captain."

"Could this being present a danger to the ship?"

"Possible . . . quite possible, sir."

Kirk was at the elevator. "Lieutenant Uhura, notify Security to have a detachment, armed and ready, to beam down with us. Stay hooked on to us. Let's go, Mr. Spock. If any word from Star Fleet Command comes through, pipe it down at once. Communications priority one."

"Aye, sir."

For a planet capable of such violent mood changes, it was extraordinarily Earth-like. It was arid, hot and dry, the terrain where the landing group materialized resembling one of Earth's desert expanses. When Spock, studying his tricorder, pointed to the left, they moved off. Almost at once they met up with huge, tumbled boulders of granite, the passageways among then littered with rocky debris. They were edging through one of the defiles when they saw it.

At the base of a cliff lay a cone-shaped craft. It was like no spaceship any of them had ever seen. Its hull was studded with buttons connected to a mesh of coiling electronic circuits. Nothing moved around it. Its wedge-like door was open. Spock stood to one side as Kirk peered inside it. Its interior was a mass of complex instrumentation, shining wirings, tubes of unrecognizable purple metal, parabolic reflectors. There was what appeared to be a control panel. A chair.

Kirk emerged, his face puzzled. "I've never seen anything like it. Have a look, Mr. Spock. . . ."

Spock was stepping through the door when the voice spoke. "You came! Thank God! There's still time!"

Everyone whirled, phasers out. Kirk looked up. On the cliff above them stood a man. He wore a ripped and disheveled jumper suit. He was a big man, but his face had been badly battered. A dark bruise had swollen his jaw. A husky man, but his broad shoulders sagged with an unutterable weariness. "It's not too late!" he cried down to them. "We can still stop him!" He extended his hands in appeal. "But I . . . I need your help . . . please . . . help me . . ."

He reeled, clutching at his throat. Then his knees buckled—and he tumbled, headlong, from the cliff.

Kirk and Spock ran to him. His body lay unmoving but massive physical power was still latent in it. Who was he? What were he and his spacecraft doing on this "routine" planet?

But McCoy would permit no questions. He shook his head over the bed in Sickbay, where the injured castaway had been placed. "It's going to be touch and go, Jim. Heartbeat practically nonexistent. What happened down there?"

"I don't know. He fell from a cliff. He'd been saying something about needing our help . . . and he just crumpled."

McCoy looked up from his diagnostic tricorder. "No wonder. After the beating he's taken."

"He was beaten?"

"I don't know what else could have caused his injuries."

"Bones," Kirk said, "that is a dead, lifeless, arid planet down there . . . no sign of living beings. Who could have attacked him?"

McCoy was frowning at his tricorder. "He's the only one who can answer that—if he lives. . . ."

They both turned at the sound of Uhura's voice on the intercom. "Captain. Standby notice just in from Star Fleet Command. Red Two message about to come in."

"I'm on my way." At the door he said, "Keep me posted, Bones."

Chemist Charlene Masters met him at the bridge elevator door. "Here's my report on the di-lithium crystals, sir. Whatever that phenomenon was, it drained almost all of our crystals' power. It could mean trouble."

"You have a talent for understatement, Lieutenant. Without full crystal power, our orbit will begin to decay in ten hours. Reamplify immediately."

"Aye, sir."

He handed the report back to her and crossed to Spock's station. "Any further magnetic disturbance, Mr. Spock?"

"Negative, Captain. Scanners indicate situation normal."

"Nothing?"

"Nothing, sir. And most illogical . . . an effect of that proportion incapable of explanation by any established physical laws I'm aware of." He paused. "I *have* ascertained one fact. Though the effect, whatever it was, was unquestionably widespread, it was strongest on the planet below us."

"Keep checking."

"Yes, Captain."

Uhura spoke. "Captain. Message coming in from Star Fleet Command. And the code, sir, it's Code Factor One."

The anxiety in her face reflected Kirk's sense of personal shock. Very seldom indeed did Star Fleet resort to Code Factor One to transmit a message. "Repeat," he told Uhura.

She said heavily, "It *is* Code Factor One, sir."

THE ALTERNATIVE FACTOR 5

"Combat status!" Kirk shouted to Spock. He hit his communicator button. "All hands! This is the Captain. Battle stations! This is not a drill! Lieutenant Uhura, the main screen!"

"Aye, sir."

Sirens were shrieking as Kirk rushed to his command position. Over the noise his communicator beeped. It was McCoy. "About our patient, Jim—"

"Quickly, Bones!"

"He'll make it. He'll be flat on his back for at least a month. He's weak as a kitten but he'll pull through."

"Thank you, Bones. I'll be down to talk to him later. The message, Lieutenant Uhura . . ."

The strong face of Commodore Barstow came into focus on the screen.

"Kirk here, sir. *Enterprise* standing by."

The official voice spoke. "You're aware, Captain, of that effect that occurred an hour ago?"

"Yes, sir."

"You may not be aware of its scope. It was felt in every quadrant of the galaxy . . . and far beyond. Complete disruption of normal magnetic and gravimetric fields. Time warp distortion. Impossible radiation variations—and all of them centering in the area you are now patrolling. The question is . . . are they natural phenomena—or are they mechanically created? And if they are . . . by whom? For what pupose? Your guess, Captain . . ."

"My best guess, sir, is . . . because of the severity of the phenomena . . . they could be a prelude to an extra-universe invasion."

"Exactly our consensus. It's your job to make the finding specific."

"Aye, sir. Can you assign me other Starships as a reserve force?"

"Negative. I am evacuating all Star Fleet units and personnel within a hundred parsecs of your position. It's tough on you and the *Enterprise*—but that's the card you've drawn. You're on your own, Captain."

Kirk spoke slowly. "I see. You mean . . . we're the bait."

"Yes."

"I understand, sir. Received and recorded."

"Remember, you're the eyes and ears and muscle of the entire Federation. Good luck, Captain."

"Thank you, sir."

The screen's image faded. Kirk looked at the blankness for a long moment. Then he rose and crossed to Spock. "From the top, Mr. Spock. First, we know that the phenomena came from the planet below us. Second, that the danger is real and imminent."

"A closer examination of the surface would seem to be in order," Spock said. "My job, Captain?"

"Yes. And in the meantime I'll have a talk with our unexpected guest. Maybe he can provide some answers."

He certainly seemed able to provide them. In Sickbay, Kirk found McCoy staring dazedly at his patient. The man who'd been nearly pushed through the door of death was out of bed, doing deep knee bends while he inhaled great hearty gulps of air. Kirk stopped in mid-stride. "Bones! I thought you said—"

McCoy struggled to come out of his daze. "I know what I said and I was going to call you back . . . but Lazarus—"

"Aye!" shouted the patient. "Lazarus! Up and out of the grave! Hale, hearty and drunk with the wine of victory!"

If the man was mentally sick, he was surely in great physical shape. He had swiftly noted the dubious look on Kirk's face. "You want to know how I came to be down there, Captain? I'll tell you! I was pursuing the devil's own spawn—the thing I have chased across the universe! Oh, he's a humanoid, all right, outside—but on the inside, he's a ravening, murderous monster! But I'll get him yet! I've sworn it!"

"Why?" Kirk said.

The eyes under the heavy brows flamed. "The beast destroyed my entire civilization! To the last man, woman and child! Builders, educators, scientists—all my people! But he missed me. And I will bring him down! Yes, despite his weapons!"

Kirk said, "How did you escape?"

THE ALTERNATIVE FACTOR

"I was inspecting our magnetic communication satellites, a thousand miles out."

"And he destroyed your whole civilization?" Kirk was openly incredulous.

"Oh, he's capable of it!" Lazarus assured him. "He's intelligent—I give him his due! But he is death! Anti-life! He lives to destroy! You believe me, don't you, Captain?"

"Just before we found you," Kirk said, "this ship sustained a number of dangerous and incredible effects. Could this humanoid of yours have been responsible?"

"Of course! It's what I've been telling you!"

He'd wanted an answer. Now he'd gotten one. If it wasn't too satisfying, it was the only one yet available. Lazarus seized on his hesitation. "Then you're with me!" he cried triumphantly. "You'll join my holy cause! You'll help me visit justice upon him—vengeance!"

"My sole cause is the security of my ship," Kirk said. "That and the mission it has undertaken. Bloodshed is not our cause. Remember that." He paused. "Now I want you to beam down to the surface with me. We shall check out your story."

They found Spock examining the conical craft's interior. Two crewmen were busy surveying its hull with tricorders.

"Find anything, Mr. Spock?" Kirk asked.

"Negative, Captain." Spock gestured toward Lazarus. "Did you?"

"According to our unexpected guest there's a creature of some sort down here—a humanoid."

Spock nodded. "Lieutenant Uhura communicated that information. I ordered reconfirmation on our sensors. They indicate no living creature on this planet. I suggest, Captain, that you have been lied to."

Kirk shot a hard look at Lazarus. Then he said, "Let's hear the rest of it, Mr. Spock."

"Lieutenant Uhura added his statement about some unusual weapon system at the humanoid's disposal."

"Aye!" yelled Lazarus. "He has that—and more! Enough to destroy a vessel as great as your *Enterprise!*"

"Does he?" Spock said mildly.

Lazarus was visibly irritated. "Yes," he said shortly.

Spock spoke to Kirk. "There are no weapons of any kind on the planet, Captain. Not in his craft. Nor on the surface. They do not exist."

"You must not believe him, Captain! This one of the pointed ears is just trying to disguise his own incompetence!"

Spock raised an eyebrow. "I don't understand your indignation, sir. I merely made the logical deduction that you are a liar."

Kirk wheeled sharply on Lazarus. "All right, let's have it! The truth this time. I—" He stopped. The air around them suddenly broke into shimmering sparkle. There came a sound like the buzzing of an angry bee. As though to ward it off, Lazarus lifted a hand. Then he fisted it, shaking it wildly at the sky. "You've come back then, is that it?" he shouted. "Well, don't stop! Here I am! Come at me again! We'll finish it!"

Ignoring him, Kirk spoke to Spock. "Can your tricorder identify that atmospheric effect?"

"It's—" Spock was saying when Lazarus bolted off to where the glitter sparkled most strongly. "Run! Run!" he screamed. "It will do you no good! I'll chase you into the very jaws of hell!"

"Lazarus!" Kirk cried. He raced after the man, calling back over his shoulder, "Remain there! All personnel on Security Red!"

He brought up in a rock-walled gully. Ahead of him Lazarus was clambering over its jagged debris. He was moving slowly when the shimmering sparkle engulfed him. At the same moment, Kirk saw that the sky, the rocks and the gully itself were trembling, shifting into indistinctness, their colors, their shapes, their masses liquefying and interflowing. They came into focus again. But Lazarus had staggered backward—and once more the liquefying shimmer had swallowed up the sight of him.

Flailing helplessly, he had tumbled into a peculiar tunnel. It was filled with a ghastly milky whiteness into which walls, roof and floor were constantly dissolving, leaving no solid point of reference required by humankind to determine its place in the universe. Unheard by Kirk, he shrieked, *"You!"* Then the manlike thing was on him. In deadly combat, they writhed, twisted together, hands grop-

THE ALTERNATIVE FACTOR

ing for each other's throats. Lazarus was choking, when he made a supreme effort, mu... ing with strain. His assailant was thrown back disappeared into the drifting whiteness.

Reeling drunkenly, Lazarus staggered out of the tunnel into Kirk's sight. Before Kirk could reach him, he fell, striking his head against a boulder. He struggled up to his hands and knees, his face streaked with blood and sweat. Kirk ran to him.

"Lazarus! Where were you? What happened?"

Horror moved in the dazed eyes. "I . . . saw it again! The Thing! It attacked me. . . ."

"I'll take you back. Hold on to me."

As he was hefting the man to his feet, Spock came through the gully. He hurried to them but Lazarus pushed away his supporting arm. Stepping aside, Spock said, "That effect occurred again, Captain. And it centered right here . . . almost where we are standing."

Lazarus lifted his head. "I told you! It was the Thing! All whiteness . . . emptiness . . ."

Kirk wiped his face clear of its blood and sweat. "There's nothing you can do about it here. We're beaming back to the ship."

The man tried to wrench himself free of Kirk's grasp. "We must kill him first! He tried to kill me! Don't you understand? If we don't stop him, he will kill us all!"

As Kirk watched McCoy apply a dressing to the deep cut on his guest's forehead, doubt of the humanoid's existence continued to trouble him. He had not seen the humanoid. He had not seen the fight. Both had been invisible to him. All he had to go on was the word of Lazarus. He felt a sudden need to confer with Spock. There was a climate of controlled tension in the bridge as he entered it. At Spock's station he lowered his voice.

"Any luck, Mr. Spock?"

"Negative, Captain. I can no more explain the second phenomenon than I can the first."

"If there's a shred of truth in what Lazarus said—"

"That a humanoid—a single creature—could be responsible for an effect of such magnitude?"

"Hard to credit," Kirk said.

"Indeed, sir."

"But the rest of his tale seems to fit. His wounds testify to an apparent confrontation with *something*."

"Affirmative, sir."

Kirk took three restless paces and came back. "Then, assuming there is a humanoid, *how* does he cause the effects? He has no weapons, no power system..."

"I'm sorry, Captain. All I know for certain is that the occurrence of the phenomena seems to coincide exactly with the moments Lazarus has one of his alleged confrontations."

Uhura interrupted them. "Doctor McCoy, Captain, asking for you in Sickbay. He says it's urgent."

McCoy was troubled too. He was at his desk, drumming it impatiently with his fingers. "Jim, maybe I'm suffering from delusions; maybe I'm not. You tell me."

"No, Bones. You tell me. That's why I'm here."

McCoy swung around. "Thirty minutes ago you brought Lazarus here and I treated a deep abrasion on his forehead. Right?"

"Right."

"I treated that wound, bandaged it, then stepped in here for a moment."

"The point, Bones."

"Say he's got a constitution like a dinosaur. Recuperative powers ditto—and as we both know, I'm a bright young medic with a miraculous touch. But tell me this. Why, when I returned to my patient, wasn't there a trace of that wound on his forehead? Not even a bruise, Jim. It was as though he'd never been injured!"

Kirk was silent for a long moment. Then he said, "Where is he?"

"I'm just a country doctor, not a private detective. Maybe he stepped out for a cup of coffee...."

But his goal was the *Enterprise* Recreation Room. Spock found him sitting at a table, quietly enjoying himself as he watched two crewmen playing a game. There was no bandage on his forehead. Spock moved to him. "May I sit down?"

He seemed to have recovered from his antagonism. "Yes, of course," he said.

"Earlier," Spock said, "I referred to you as a liar."

"Do you still think I am?"

"About some matters, yes."

Lazarus smiled. "You're very direct. I like that. If it will help make up your mind about me, ask your questions."

"I am curious about this civilization of yours . . . the one that was destroyed."

"It was much like that of Earth. Green, soft landscapes, blue seas, great cities, science, education. . . ."

"And the people?"

"Like any of us. Good, bad, beautiful, ugly, magnificent . . . terrible. Human. Satisfied?"

"The story you have told us is most strange and unlikely, as you yourself. You are hardly the same man I spoke to earlier."

"Don't blame me if I'm not consistent, Mr. Spock. Not even the universe is that."

"I prefer to think it is," Spock said.

He got a sharp stare. "Yes. Of course you would."

The wall communicator beeped. Spock got up and went to it. "Yes, Lieutenant Uhura?"

"You told me to notify you when the impulse readings reached the critical stage. They've done so."

"Thank you, Lieutenant." He returned to Lazarus. "If you will excuse me, I have an experiment in progress— one that may help me evaluate the facts."

"When you are certain of your facts, will you believe me then?"

"I always believe in facts, sir." He eyed the unbandaged forehead. "I must congratulate you on your remarkable recuperative powers. If time permitted, I would like to discuss them with you." He bowed. "Thank you for your company."

Lazarus was watching him leave when the shimmer suddenly sparkled again. He half-rose from the table, went pallid and almost fell from his chair. The sparkle subsided; and controlling his shaking knees, he moved out into the corridor. The effect came again. The corridor walls faded, dissolving. Then they were back, solid, real. Staring about, Lazarus hauled himself up from where he had fallen. On his forehead was the white tape marking the wound he had received on the planet. He heard Kirk call, "Lazarus!"

McCoy saw him first. They rushed to him, Kirk taking his arm. "Are you all right?"

"What? Oh, yes, Captain. All right! But impatient! Have you decided to help me yet?"

McCoy was staring at him. He stepped forward, seized the edge of the tape and pulled it off. There was a red, neatly sliced cut in the bruised forehead.

"Well . . ." McCoy said.

Kirk, too, had his eyes fixed on the deep cut.

"Something wrong, Captain?" Lazarus asked.

Kirk glanced at McCoy. "No. Except that I have a ship's physician with a strange sense of humor."

McCoy wheeled. "Jim, this is no joke! I know what I saw!"

The wall communicator beeped. "Bridge. Calling the Captain."

Kirk hit the switch. "Kirk here."

Spock said, "Request you come up, sir."

"Find something?"

"Something quite extraordinary, Captain."

"On my way." He turned a cold eye on Lazarus. "You will come with me. I have some questions still to be answered."

Spock had ordered activation of the main viewing screen. It showed the planet flaring with a single needle point of blinking light. Spock joined Kirk. "A source of radiation, Captain."

"Why didn't our scanners pick it up before?"

"Because it isn't there," Spock said.

Kirk could feel the tension hardening in his midriff. "A riddle, Mr. Spock? First Bones, now you."

"What I meant, sir—is, according to usual scanning procedure, there is nothing there that could be causing the phenomenon."

"But the radiation point *is* there."

"Affirmative, sir." Spock hesitated. "I confess I am somewhat at a loss for words. It may be best described, though loosely and inaccurately . . . as a—" He paused again, his embarrassment to be read only in the particular impassivity of his face. "As . . . a 'rip' in our universe."

"A *what?*"

"A peculiar physical warp, Captain, in which none of our established physical laws seem to apply with regularity. It was only with our di-lithium crystals that I was able to localize it."

Lazarus burst into speech. "Of course! The di-lithium crystals! Their power—that could do it!" He whirled to Kirk with a wild shout. "We've got him now, Captain! We've got him!"

"You refer to the humanoid?" Spock inquired.

"Yes! By the gods, *yes!* Now we have him!"

"What have the crystals got to do with it? All they show is a point of radiation," Kirk said.

"But that's it! That's the key—the solution! That's how we can trap him! I implore you . . . I beg you . . . I demand—*give me those crystals!*"

Kirk shook his head. "Out of the question. The crystals are the very heart of my ship's power."

The eyes that glared at him were congested with blood. "Fool, don't you understand? There'll *be* no ship unless this monster is killed! He'll destroy all of you!"

Kirk gritted his teeth. "How, Lazarus? *How?* All I've heard from you is doubletalk—lies—threats that never materialize—explanations that don't hold a drop of water! Now you tell me—*how is my ship in danger? How?*"

The face tightened into hard determination. Lazarus turned and started toward the elevator.

Kirk shouted his name. The man whirled around, fury distorting his heavy features. "I warn you, Captain—you will give me the crystals!"

Kirk spoke very quietly. "Don't threaten me."

"I'm not threatening you. I am telling you I will have my vengeance!" The elevator whirred open and he was gone.

Kirk's tension had broken into open rage. He turned to a guard. "Security! From now on he's your job—your *only* job! If he does anything, tries to—anything at all unusual—notify me at once!"

The guard was already moving toward the elevator.

In the Engineering section Charlene Masters was directing the procedure required to recharge the di-lithium crystals. She had opened one of the bins when her assistant turned from the intercom. "Lieutenant Masters," he said, "the Captain is calling."

She moved off to the far wall. As she turned her back, a figure edged from the shadow behind the bins toward the assistant. A powerful arm encircled the man's neck, applying hard pressure to the throat. Then quietly, almost tenderly, it eased him to the ground.

The oblivious Charlene was listening to Kirk say, "Can you prepare an experimentation chamber in ten minutes? All di-lithium crystals full power, Lieutenant."

"I'll check, sir." She returned to the bins for readings and went back to the intercom. "Captain? Chamber will be ready in ten minutes. My assistant and I—".

A hand clamped over her mouth. Kirk heard her choking gurgle. "Lieutenant Masters? Masters, what's wrong?"

She managed to wrench her head free for a brief instant. "Captain. . . . .!" Her eyes were glazing as she was dropped to the deck.

The Lazarus of the powerful arm bore no sign of a cut on his forehead.

It was a furious Kirk who called the meeting in the Briefing Room. Lazarus, the red wound back on his forehead, sat at the head of the table. Kirk paced up and down behind his chair, his eyes on the blackening finger marks on Charlene Masters' throat. He waited for Spock to enter before he spoke.

"Two of my crewmen have been attacked—*and two of our di-lithium crystals are missing!* Without them this ship cannot operate at full power. They must be found!"

He seized the back of the chair Lazarus sat in. Wheeling around, he shouted, "Fact! You said you needed those crystals! Fact! Within an hour after telling me you must have them, *they are missing!*"

Lazarus half-rose from the chair. "And fact!" he cried. *"I didn't take the crystals!"*

His head drooped. "I'm not the one, Captain," he said

quietly. "In me the *Enterprise* found only an orphan. . . . Find my enemy. Find the beast—and you'll find your crystals!"

"And just how did your beast get aboard my ship?"

"He has ways! There's no end to his evil!"

Kirk looked at Spock. "If the creature transported up—"

"Lazarus laughed. "Transport *up?* I tell you, we are dealing with a Thing capable of destroying worlds! He has your crystals!"

"But why, sir?" Spock asked mildly. "Again we must put the question to you. For what purposes?"

Lazarus leaped from his chair. "The same as mine! Why don't you listen to me? He's humanoid! He can operate a ship! Compute formulas to exterminate a race! Strangle a man with his bare hands! Or steal an energy source for his vehicle in order to escape me! Are you deaf as well as blind?"

There was something wrong. Trust of this man was impossible to come by. The frustration piled up in Kirk until his fists clenched. "Mr. Spock, the crystals certainly aren't here. There is an unexplained source of radiation on the planet. There is clearly some connection. We'll check it out. Prepare a search party at once. Mr. Lazarus will beam down with us."

Lazarus smiled. "Thank you, Captain."

Kirk's voice was harsh. "You may not have reason to thank me. That will depend on what we find."

The cone-shaped craft still lay at the base of the cliff. As Kirk opened its door, Lazarus went to him. "Now what do you believe, Captain?"

"I believe the missing crystals are not in your ship. Mr. Spock?"

"Unable to locate the radiation source, sir."

"Why not? You had it spotted from the ship."

"It simply seems to have disappeared."

Kirk spoke to the guards. "I want every inch of this terrain checked. Look for footprints, movement, anything. If you spot something, call out. And don't be afraid to use your weapons."

The party fanned out over the terrain, each man at once becoming aware of its empty loneliness. No trees, no vegetation—just the unfolding vista of rock in its multiple formations. Lazarus climbed to a craggy ridge, spined like an emaciated dinosaur petrified by the eons. Along its left slope glacial boulders balanced precariously over a steepness that dropped to a long defile. It ran parallel to the ridge; and Kirk, his tricorder out, was exploring it. Lazarus, lost to sight between two jutting rocks, clutched at one as the space around him began to shimmer. In the hideous sparkle, the rocks, the sky, the very ground under his feet seemed to fade and melt. He spun around, peering for his enemy. But there was only the shimmering nothingness. He found that his movement was slowed down. Stumbling forward, he lurched into a milky-white cocoon place—and a blow struck him to his knees. Vaporlike stuff was in his eyes, his nose, his throat. The vague shape of his assailant leaped on him. They wrestled blindly, bits of the stuff drifting over them. Lazarus kicked the thing. It fell back and vanished as though it had dropped into eternity.

Then the world was solid again. Lazarus careened wildly, still fighting off the absent enemy. He tripped against a rock at the edge of the ridge. It teetered. Lunging forward, he shouted, *"Captain! Look out!"*

Kirk leaped aside. And the massive rock crashed into the defile where he'd been moving the moment before. Then the edge of the ridge crumbled. Lazarus fell at Kirk's feet.

When Spock found them, dust was still drifting down on both men.

McCoy had a stretcher waiting in the Transporter Room. Lazarus was still unconscious. In Sickbay his recovery came hard. Kirk saw the horror twist his face as he struggled back into awareness. He tried to leap from the examining table.

"The Thing!" he cried hoarsely.

"You're on the *Enterprise* now," Kirk said. "Doctor McCoy says you'll be all right."

"How's your head?" McCoy asked.

A hand touched the cut forehead. "It aches."

"You saved my life down there," Kirk said. "I thank

you for that." He paused. "But I have to ask you some questions."

"Jim! A possible concussion—"

"It's necessary!" Kirk flared.

"Go ahead, Captain," Lazarus said.

"I am holding," Kirk said, "a computer report on the information you gave us during your initial screening. It calls you a liar, Lazarus. For one thing, there is no planet at the location you claimed to have come from. There never has been."

Lazarus sat up, his eyes on Kirk's face. "You wouldn't believe the truth if I told it to you," he said slowly.

"Try us," Kirk said.

"About my home planet . . . I distorted a fact in the interest of self-preservation and my sacred cause. You, too, are a stranger to me, Captain—an unknown factor." He swung his legs from the table, making a tentative effort to stand.

"I needed help, not censure," he said. "Freedom, not confinement as a madman. If I told you the truth, I feared that was what you'd call me."

"The truth now, if you please," Kirk said.

Lazarus looked at him, his deep passion thickening his voice. "All right, sir! My planet, my home—or what's left of it—is down there below us!"

Kirk stared at him, dumbfounded. "What are you saying?"

"That my space ship is more than a space ship. It is also a time chamber . . . a time ship. And I, if you will, am a time traveler."

Kirk frowned. This man was a compounder of mysteries. All he had told were lies . . . and yet that vessel of his, like nothing before seen on heaven or earth, its unrecognizable complexities. . . . He spoke tonelessly. "And this thing you search for? Is it a time traveler, too?"

The eyes went wild. "Yes! He's fled me across all the years, all the empty years! To a dead future on the dead planet he murdered!" He was feverish now, staggering to his feet. "Help me, man! You have more crystals! Give me the tools I need to kill him!" He tottered and McCoy grabbed him. He wrenched free of the supporting arm.

"The crystals! What are they to the abomination I hunt? What is anything compared to its supernal evil? Do you want him to get away?"

"Lazarus, there are a lot of things going on that we know nothing about. But *you* know. Now tell me—*where are our crystals?*"

"I told you!" Lazarus shouted. "He has them! He took them!"

They had to ease him back on the table or he would have fallen. He lay there, prone, his eyes glassy, face streaming with sweat. McCoy said, "He's got to rest, Jim. And would you mind getting that muscle man out of my Sickbay?"

Nodding, Kirk dismissed the guard. Uneasy, he watched McCoy cover Lazarus with a sheet. There was a deep sigh and the eyes closed. "He's in a lot of pain, Jim."

"Pain," Kirk said. "Sometimes it can drive a man harder than pleasure." He looked at the face on the table. It was whiter than the sheet. "But I guess he won't be going anywhere for a while—not this time."

As the door closed behind them, the sheeted form moved. The eyes opened. Grasping the table, Lazarus hauled himself to his feet. He faltered, shaking his head to clear it. Then, cautiously, stealthily, motored by his inexorable determination, he moved to the door.

Kirk chose the Briefing Room to put the Big Questions to Spock. He turned from his restless pacing to cry, "But just what have we got? A magnetic effect which produces your 'wink-out' phenomenon. And a mysterious, unidentifiable source of radiation on the planet. Lazarus, a walking powder-keg. Your 'rip' in the universe. That murdering humanoid none of us have seen..."

Spock looked up from his computer tie-in. "True, Captain. But what is significant to me is the fact that our ship's instruments are specifically designed to locate and identify any physical object in the universe, whether it be matter or energy."

"But using them you were unable to identify that source of radiation on the planet!"

"Correct, sir."

"Are the instruments in order?"

"In perfect operating condition."

"Then what you say leaves only one conclusion. The source of that radiation is not of our universe."

"Nor in it, Captain. It came from outside."

Kirk resumed his pacing. "Yes—outside of it. That would explain a lot! Another universe . . . perhaps in another dimension . . . but occupying the same space at the same time."

"The possibility of the existence of a parallel universe has been scientifically conceded, Captain."

"All right. What would happen if another universe, say a minus universe, came into contact with a positive one such as ours?"

"Unquestionably a warp, Captain. A distortion of physical laws on an immense scale."

"That's what we have been experiencing! The point where they touch—couldn't it be described as a hole?"

Their two minds seemed to meet and meld. Spock nodded vigorously. "Indeed, Captain. I also point out that a hole in the universe—or in a simple container—can either allow the contents to escape or—"

"What is outside to enter it!" Kirk shouted. "Mr. Spock, the invasion that Commodore Barstow suspected!"

"There is no evidence of any large-scale invasion, sir."

"But a small-scale invasion! Spock! What's your evaluation of the mental state of Lazarus?"

"At one moment, paranoid. But the next, calm, rational, mild. Almost as if he were—" Spock paused on the edge of light. "Almost as if he were two men."

"Exactly! Two men—different but identical. And a hole in the universe! No! Not a hole! A door, Spock, a door!"

"You *are* hypothesizing a parallel universe, Captain!"

"And why not? It's theoretically possible! Look at Lazarus! One minute he's at the point of death . . . but the next alive and well, strong as a bull. That cut on his forehead. First he has it, then it's gone—and then he has it again! For one man it's all physically impossible!"

"I agree, Captain. There are unquestionably two of him."

"But . . . what's going on? This leaping from one universe to the other? The wild rant about a murdering thing that destroys civilizations! What's the purpose?"

"Captain, madness has no purpose. No reason. But—it could have a goal!" Spock's face was stony as his Vulcan blood triumphed over his human agitation. "He must be stopped, Captain! Destroyed, if necessary."

"Spock, I'm not following you now."

"Two universes, sir! Project this! One positive, one negative. Or, more specifically, one of them matter—and the other one, antimatter!"

Kirk regarded him for a tense moment. "But matter and antimatter—they cancel one another out . . . violently."

"Precisely . . . under certain conditions. When identical particles of matter and antimatter meet—identical, Captain, like—"

"Like Lazarus—like the two of them. Identical, except that one is matter and the other antimatter. And if they meet . . ."

Kirk had never heard Spock's voice so somber. "Annihilation, Captain. Total, complete, annihilation . . ."

"And of everything that exists . . . everywhere. . . ."

It was a moment for failure in speech. They stared at each other as the fate of worlds, known and unknown, dropped itself into their laps.

Lazarus found the corridor deserted. He turned the corner that led to Engineering; and sidling through its door, went swiftly to an electrical relay panel. Its maze of wires struck him as primitive. It took him barely a moment to remove a tool from his jumper suit, detach a connection and affix the wire to a different terminal. Closing the panel, he waited, a shadow in the darker shadow behind a throbbing dynamo.

Far to his left, Charlene Masters was studying the effect of recharge on her di-lithium crystals. Above the bins the needle of a thermometerlike device had wavered up toward a red mark. It climbed above it—and a wisp of smoke drifted up from one of the lower dials. She looked away from the installation to examine the chart held by her assistant. They smelled the smoke at the same time. "The energizer! It's shorted!" she cried.

There was a flashing spray of sparks. A great, billowing cloud of smoke engulfed them. "Get out of here, Ensign! Sound the alarm!" She was coughing.

"You, too, Lieutenant!"

"No! I've got to—"

"You've got to get out of here!" he shouted. "The whole bank might blow!" He seized her arm, dragging her through the still-thickening smoke. Half-blinded, choking, they staggered out into the corridor. As they passed him, Lazarus, a piece of torn sheet held over his nose and mouth, shut the door quietly behind them.

Charlene was at the wall communicator. "Engineering! Fire! Energizing circuits!"

Uhura whirled from her board. "Fire, Captain! Engineering! Situation critical!"

"All available hands, Lieutenant! On the double! Spock! On me!"

The Ensign, still coughing, his face black-streaked, met them at the door to Engineering. "Under control, sir. But it couldn't have— Captain, that fire did not start by itself!"

Spock said, "Lazarus, Captain? A ruse? To get at the di-lithium crystals?"

"Way ahead of you, Mr. Spock."

They both plunged into the smoky room. Coughing, Kirk groped his way to the bins. "He's got them all right. And he's beaming down right now. I'm going after him. Get together a Security detail. Follow me as soon as you can."

"Aye, aye, sir."

Lazarus had tied the crystals in the torn sheet. Materialized, he hurried directly to his craft. In its working area, he unwrapped them exultantly. Shaking his fist at his invisible foe, he yelled, "Now I'll do it. I have a threshold! Run! Run! I've got you now!"

Bending to his labor, he selected certain rods and wires that soon assumed the shape of a protective frame before the ship's entrance. He worked quickly, arranging what were obviously premade units. In them he carefully placed the di-lithium crystals. When the last one was safely installed, he raised his fists skyward, howling like a wolf, "It's done! It's finished! Finished!"

Kirk, nearing the ship, heard him. Phaser extended, he said, "Wrong, Lazarus. *You're* finished. Through. Back up!" He stepped through the door.

"No!" Lazarus shrieked.

The warning came too late. The shimmering sparkles flared. Kirk vanished.

Lazarus, head huddled in his arms, cried, "No! Not you! *Not you!*"

For Kirk, banished into the tunnel of negative magnetism, time and space died. He was spinning in a kind of slow motion where familiar time was boundless and empty space stuff that broke off against his face in fluffy hunks. He was falling but he was also rising. He was twisting while at the same time he lay still. The nightmare of an absolute disorientation was crawling over him. The shimmer shimmered. It faded—and he found himself on his hands and knees, fighting nausea.

Vaguely, with disinterest, he saw rocks, gullies, the old dry desolation, the cliff that sheltered the time craft. The ship was gone. There was no sign of it—no sign of anything or anybody. He got slowly to his feet, staring at the cliff base where the craft should have been. After a moment, he hefted the phaser in his hand, unsure that it was real. It was—solid, real against his palm. He looked around again before he called, "Hello!"

The word echoed back from the rocks. Then only the silence spoke.

He took off at a run up a slope. It gave on to a plateau. The time craft was there, set in a little open space, but no sign of life about it. Then the Lazarus of the uncut forehead rose from his stooping position. He, too, was rigging some kind of framework before the ship's entrance. He smiled at the aimed phaser. "Welcome, Captain. I wasn't expecting you."

"No," Kirk said. *"Him."*

"You understand then?"

"Not completely. This is clearly a parallel universe."

"Of course."

"Antimatter?"

"Here, yes."

"And if identical particles meet . . ."

"The end of everything, Captain. Of creation. Of existence. All gone." He squared his broad shoulders. "I'm trying to stop him. It's why I took your di-lithium crystals."

"He has two more."

Lazarus searched Kirk's face. "That's very bad, Captain. If he can come through, at a time of his own choosing. But I think, if we hurry . . . and you will help me, he can yet be stopped. But we have little time."

It was Spock who materialized before the other time ship, still at the foot of the cliff. The matter Lazarus, the wound on his forehead, stood at its door, violently waving his arms. "Back! Back!" he screamed. "If you ever want to see your Captain alive again, get back!"

"Do what he says," Spock told his Security guards.

Up on the plateau, the second Lazarus had his threshold frame almost completed. He pointed to a tool; and as Kirk handed it to him, he said, "He meant to come through this but when you accidentally contacted it, it drained his crystals. It will take him at least ten minutes to re-energize with the equipment on board his craft. That should give us time enough. . . ."

"Just exactly what did I contact?" Kirk said.

"I call it the alternative warp, Captain. It's the negative magnetic corridor where the parallel universes come together. It's . . . the safety valve. It keeps eternity from blowing up."

"This corridor," Kirk said. "Is it what caused the magnetic effect—that sort of 'wink-out' phenomenon?"

"Precisely, Captain. But not because of its existence. Only because *he* entered it. The corridor is like a jail with explosives attached to its door. Open the door—and the explosives may detonate. Stay inside the corridor—"

"And the universe is safe," Kirk said.

"Your universe and mine, Captain. Both of them."

"Surely he must know what would happen if he ever does meet you face to face outside that corridor."

"Of course he knows. But he is mad, Captain. You've heard him. His mind is gone. When our people found the way to slip through the warp . . . when they proved the existence of another identical universe, it was too much for him. He could not live, knowing that I lived. He became obsessed with passion to destroy me. The fact that my death would also destroy him—and everything else—cannot matter to him."

Kirk spoke slowly. "So you're the terrible Thing . . . the murdering monster . . . the creature of evil. . . ."

"Yes. Or he is. It depends on the point of view, doesn't it?"

He made a final adjustment. "It's ready, Captain. If we can force him into the corridor while I'm there waiting for him, we can put an end to this. But if he comes through the warp at a time of his own choosing—and breaks into this universe to find me . . ."

"I understand," Kirk said. "What do you want me to do?"

"Find him. Force him through his threshold frame and into the corridor. I'll be waiting. I'll hold him there."

Kirk's face had fallen into very sober lines. "You can't hold him forever."

"Can't I, Captain? You are to destroy his ship."

"But if I do that—won't this one also be destroyed?"

"It will."

"And that door—that warp—will be closed to you."

"Yes. But it will be closed to him, too."

"You'll be trapped with him," Kirk said. "You'll be trapped with him in that corridor forever . . . at each other's throats . . . throughout the rest of time."

"Is it such a large price to pay for the safety of two universes?"

Lazarus reached out and placed Kirk within the frame of his threshold. "The safety of two universes." Kirk looked at the brave man. "Are you sure you want me to do this?"

"You must do it, Captain. We have no choice. Are you ready?"

Kirk's voice was steady. "I'm ready."

"Send him to me. I'll be waiting in the corridor."

He threw a switch. The shimmering sparkles tingled over Kirk's body—and he was back on the plateau, the other space craft before him. Spock ran toward him. He shook his head, waving him back.

The first Lazarus was busy at his threshold frame, his

back to Kirk. He moved a lever. The structure glowed, then flashed into glitter. "You're done!" he told it exultantly.

Kirk jumped him. But he whirled in time to block the tackle with his heavy body. Then they closed, wrestling, Kirk, silent, intent, boring in as he fought to back the man into the frame. His aim became clear to Lazarus. *"No!"* he yelled. "You can't! I'm not ready! Not now! Not yet!" He seized a thick metal tool for bludgeon. Kirk ducked the blow, rising fast to connect a hard fist to his jaw. Lazarus wavered; and Kirk held him, pushing, pushing him backward until he stumbled, toppling over into the frame. The sparkle caught him. There was a blinding glare of whiteness—and he was gone.

Kirk pulled in a deep lungful of breath. Spock took over. Turning to his men, he said, "Get those di-lithium crystals back to the ship. Hurry!" Then he spoke to Kirk. "Captain, am I right in guessing that this craft must be completely destroyed?"

"To the last particle."

"And what of Lazarus, sir?"

"Yes," Kirk said. "What of Lazarus, Mr. Spock?"

There was no out. And Kirk, back in his command chair, knew it. He'd chosen the Service; and if he'd been unaware of what would be required of a Starship Captain back in those long-ago Academy days, the choice was still his. Nor could any human being expect to foresee the consequences of any decision. Met up with them, all you could do was deal with them as responsibly as you could. He'd had to remind himself of this truth a thousand times—but this time...

He spoke into his intercom. "Activate phaser banks."

Somebody said, "Phaser banks activated, sir."

"Stand by to fire."

Under the words Kirk was seeing that corridor of negative magnetism. A man of solid Earth, he was remembering its frightful unearthliness, its chilling paradoxes— and he saw two men, two humans locked into it, embattled, each of them winning and losing, rising and falling, eternally victorious and eternally vanquished throughout an unbroken Forever.

He licked dry lips.

"Phasers standing by, sir."

His lips felt rough. He licked them. "Fire phasers," he said.

The beams struck the ship on the plateau. It disintegrated. Then they switched to the one at the cliff's base. It burst into flame and vanished. On the screen only the desolate landscape remained.

Solution—simple.

"Let's get out of here," Kirk said. He turned to the helmsman. "Warp one, Mr. Leslie."

"Warp one, sir."

Spock was beside him. "Everything all right, Captain?"

"It is for us, Mr. Spock."

Spock nodded. "There is, of course, no escape for them."

"No, Mr. Spock. No escape at all. How would it be to be trapped with that raging madman at your throat . . . at your throat throughout Time everlasting? How would it be?"

"But the universe is safe, Captain."

"Yes . . . for you and me. But what of Lazarus?" He paused as though posing the question to that universe Lazarus had saved.

The stars slid by the *Enterprise.* They didn't answer its Captain.

THE EMPATH

(Joyce Muskat)

The second star in the Minarian system was entering a critical period of its approaching nova phase. Accordingly, the *Enterprise* had been ordered to evacuate personnel of the research station which was established on the star to study the phenomena of its coming death. But all the Starship's attempts to contact the scientists had failed. Kirk, his urgent mission in mind, decided to beam down to the surface to try to locate their whereabouts.

He, Spock and McCoy materialized on a bleak landscape, grim and forbidding under a sky already red with the light of the imminent nova. A gust of harsh wind blew dirt in their faces. It also rattled the door of a metal hut a few yards to their right. "It's the research station," Kirk said. He led the way to it. Its door gave way under a push. The hut was deserted, but its interior, a combination of living quarters and laboratory, was neatly arranged. In a corner, Kirk spotted a video-tape recorder.

Spock ran his hand over a table. "Dust," he said. "Apparently, their instruments have not been recently in use."

The recorder still held a tape card. Kirk was about to insert it when his communicator beeped. Handing the tape to Spock, he flipped it open. It said, *"Enterprise* to Captain Kirk. Come in, please."

"Kirk here. Go ahead, *Enterprise.*"

"Scott here, Captain. Our instruments have picked up a gigantic solar flare with very high levels of cosmic rays."

"How bad?" Kirk said.

"Sensors indicate cosmic-ray concentration measures 3.51 on the Van Allen scale. It'll play the devil with the crew as well as the ship, sir."

Spock spoke. "On that basis it will take exactly 74.1 solar hours for the storm to pass, Captain."

"Warp her out of orbit right now! Mr. Scott, stay at the minimum distance for *absolute* safety!"

"Aye, aye, sir. We'll beam you up in—"

Kirk interrupted, "Negative. We're staying here. The atmosphere of the planet will protect us. Now get my ship out of danger, Mr. Scott!"

"Very well, Captain. Scott out."

"Kirk out." Closing his communicator, he turned to Spock. "Mr. Spock . . . how about that tape?"

Spock had been examining it. As he inserted it into the recorder, he said, "Whatever we see and hear, Captain, happened approximately two weeks ago."

Activated, the device's viewing screen lit up. It showed two men checking equipment against the hut's background. "The one on the left is Dr. Linke," Kirk said. "The other is Dr. Ozaba. Does the speaker work, Spock?"

It worked. Linke was saying, ". . . another week in this godforsaken place . . ."

He lurched to the shaking of a brief earthquake. Ozaba grinned. *"In His hand are the deep places of the earth.* Psalm 95, Verse 4. I wish He'd calm them down. . . ."

Abruptly, sound and picture ended. The recorder emitted a deep organlike chord. It grew louder—and the picture returned to image the scientists searching for the source of the sound. Their lips moved but their voices were overwhelmed by the rising chord's reverberation. Suddenly Ozaba clutched his head, staggering in pain. As Linke rushed forward to help him, Ozaba winked out. Terrified, Linke stared around the hut. Then he too began to stagger. He disappeared. The sound faded and the screen went blank.

Appalled, McCoy cried, "Jim, what happened to them?"

As though in answer the strange sound came again, gathering around the *Enterprise* men. Spock swiftly unlimbered his tricorder while Kirk and McCoy frantically searched for some clue to the noise.

"Where's it coming from?" Kirk shouted. "Spock, can you pin it down?"

"Negative, Captain! This 'sound' doesn't register on my tricorder!" He bent his head to check the instrument when his eyes glazed. His hands went to his head as though the increasing sound were crushing it. He reeled drunkenly. Kirk, rushing to him, put out an arm to steady him. Then Spock winked out.

Kirk stared around him in horror. The sound intensified. "Bones!" Kirk yelled. "Spock—he's gone!"

But McCoy was gripping his head. Then, he too staggered. Even as Kirk raced to him, he vanished. Stunned, Kirk stood still. The hammer of sound beat at him. He began to struggle forward like a man fighting the pull of a monstrous magnet. He stumbled against a metal staircase and fell, cutting his head. As he hauled himself back to his feet, he winked out.

The triumphant sound rose higher in the empty hut.

Time passed. How much, they never knew. But something had transported them into the center of an arenalike place. When a blinding, overhead, circular light came on, they found themselves able to move. Kirk groped up to his knees. Beyond the circle of light, the arena's boundaries were lost in total darkness. The cut on his head throbbed.

"Bones . . . Spock. Spock, where are we?"

McCoy had seen the cut. He reached for his medikit and, struggling to his feet, dealt with the injury. Spock was checking his tricorder. "We are exactly 121.32 meters below the planet's surface, Captain."

"How did we get here?"

"Residual energy readings indicate that we were beamed here by a matter-energy scrambler not dissimilar to our own Transporter mechanism."

"Is that cut very painful, Jim?"

Kirk nodded, shrugging; and Spock, his eyes still on his tricorder, said, "Captain, I'm picking up a life form . . . bearing 42 mark seven."

"Could it be one of the missing scientists?"

"Negative, sir. Although humanoid, it is definitely not *Homo sapiens.*"

"Identification?"

"Impossible. I can make no exact identification other than that it is humanoid."

"Then let's find out what it is. Phasers on stun!"

It was the tricorder that guided them through the dimness ahead. The brilliant light which had illuminated the arena's center didn't reach to its outer space. But, stumbling along it, they could finally discern what seemed to be a narrow, circular platform—a platform or a couch. On it lay a figure. It was very still.

Spock extended the tricorder. "The life form, Captain."

"What is it?" Kirk said.

The creature stirred. As it sat up, lights blazed in a sharply outlined circle over the couch. The being stood up. It had the body of a girl and it was clothed in a gossamer stuff that glittered with the sparkle of diamonds. Her skin was dead white. Dark hair clustered around her temples. But it was her eyes that riveted Kirk's. They were large, shining—the most expressive eyes he'd ever seen in his life.

McCoy started forward.

"Careful!" Kirk said sharply.

"She seems to be harmless enough, Jim."

"The sand-bats of Manark-4," Spock said, "appear to be inanimate rock crystals before they attack."

Kirk moved cautiously toward her. "I am James Kirk, Captain of the USS *Enterprise*." He gestured back to the others. "This is my Science Officer, Mr. Spock, and Doctor McCoy, Ship's Surgeon. We are not going to hurt you." He paused, still fascinated by the eyes. "Do you live here? Is this . . . your home?"

She didn't answer.

"Spock, analysis?"

"From what we know of gravity and other environmental conditions on this planet, a life form such as hers could not evolve here," McCoy said.

"Agreed, Doctor," Spock said. "She is obviously not of this planet."

"Why are you here?" Kirk asked her.

She shrugged. He persisted. "Are you responsible for bringing us here?" Despite her eyes, he was beginning to feel exasperated. "At least you must know how *you* got here!"

She shrank back. Aware that he had frightened her, Kirk relaxed. "Don't be afraid," he said gently. "You must not fear me." His reassurance didn't seem to reassure her. How should he approach this sensitive creature with the remarkable eyes? He turned to McCoy. "What about it, Bones? What's wrong with her?"

McCoy looked up from his readings. "She's mute . . . no vocal cords, not even vestigials. And it doesn't look like a pathological condition."

"Explain."

"As far as I can tell, she's perfectly healthy. As for the other, my guess is that the lack of vocal cords is physiologically normal for her species, whatever that is."

"A whole race of mutes . . . like the Gamma Vertis-4 civilization?"

"That's my opinion, for what it's worth."

"Without speech, how's she able to understand us? Unless she's a telepath. Could telepathic power have been used to bring us here?"

Spock said, "An unlikely possibility, Captain. Over ninety-eight percent of the known telepathic species send thoughts as well as receive them. She has made no attempt to contact our thoughts."

Kirk looked at her intently for a long moment. Then his hand went to his forehead, pressing tightly against its pulsing ache. As he sank down on the couch, something in the girl's white face moved McCoy to say, "We can't keep calling her 'she' as though she weren't here!"

"You have any suggestions?" Kirk said.

"I don't know about you two, but I'm going to call her 'Gem.'" Conscious of Spock's raised eyebrow, he added a defiant, "At least it's better than 'hey you'!"

Kirk got to his feet. "I want to know why we're here—what's going on. The girl may know. Spock, try the Vulcan mind meld."

Nodding, Spock went to the couch, hands extended to make contact with her. But she had watched his approach with panic. Spock, touching her arm, recoiled.

"Spock, what is it!"

"Her mind doesn't function like ours, Captain. I felt it trying to draw on *my* consciousness. Like a magnet. I could gain nothing from her."

High above their heads, like a theater's mezzanine, was a semicircular construction. And like a theater director and stage manager, placed for a different viewpoint of the actors below them, two figures were observing the little drama being enacted on the platform-stage beneath them. An organ chord sounded.

Kirk, Spock and McCoy whirled as one man.

Slowly the figures descended from their eminence. Tall, clad in floor-length robes, their bodies were muscular and agile but their faces were old, their heads bald. Among the wrinkles of great age, their eyes blazed with a purpose that was barren of all warmth or emotion. Each bore a curious silver object in his right hand. It had the shape of a T. Ignoring the men, they advanced on the cowering Gem. Again, as one man, the *Enterprise* trio moved forward protectively in front of her.

Kirk spoke. "I am——"

He was interrupted. The figure on the left said, "We are aware of your identity, Captain."

"Who are you? Why have you brought us here?"

The voice was as cold as death. "We are Vians. My name is Lal. This is Thann." A finger pointed to Gem. "Do not interfere!"

"What do you intend to do to her?"

"Delay us no longer!"

It was Thann who spoke. As he started forward, Kirk moved swiftly to block his way to the girl. Lal raised his silver T-bar and Kirk was hurled up and over her couch. The crashdown reopened the cut on his forehead. It began to bleed. Wiping blood from his eyes, he hauled himself back to his feet and, pulling out his phaser, called "Phasers on stun!" Then he circled the couch to confront the Vians. "Since you already know who we are, you must also know that we come in peace. Our prime directive specifically prohibits us from interfering with any...."

The Vians directed their T-bars at the three *Enterprise* men. Their phasers, flying out of their hands, dissolved into air. They tried to reach Gem—and a pulsing, multicolored force field enveloped them.

Thann was stooping over the girl, touching his T-bar to her head. It emitted a chilling whine. They all saw that her white face was transfixed with terror. With a concerted effort, they gathered all their strength to strain against the force field. McCoy was the first to weaken. Then it was Kirk's turn. His head swam, blurring his vision so that everything—the place, Gem, the Vians, his friends' faces, spun wildly in a vertiginous mist.

"Bones . . . I . . . can't seem to stand up. . . ."

"Stand still!" McCoy said sharply. "You too, Spock! Don't fight it, don't move! Somehow this field upsets the body metabolism. . . ."

Lal's cold eyes focused on McCoy. "Not quite, Doctor. The field draws its energy *from* your bodies. The more you resist it, the stronger it becomes."

He nodded to Thann, who moved away from Gem. When he lifted his T-bar, the chord sounded. Both Vians disappeared—and the force field collapsed so suddenly that its prisoners fell to the floor.

Kirk gritted his teeth against the pain in his head. "Mr. Spock, there must be an exit from this place. See if you can find it."

"Yes, Captain." Tricorder out, Spock moved off to quarter the arena.

"Jim, that's a nasty cut," McCoy said. "Let me have another look at it."

"Don't fuss over me, Bones. They may have hurt the girl." He went to Gem on the couch. "Did they hurt you?" he asked her.

She shook her head. Then, timidly, she touched Kirk's hands. At once pain twisted her face. She drew back; but after a moment, she raised her arm to lay a finger on his throbbing head. To his amazement he saw a cut, identical in size to his own, appear on her forehead. Marveling, he looked at the deep gash. Extending a hand, he touched it gently. It was wet with blood. She took the hand, holding it quietly. And he knew that his wound was gone. At the same instant, hers vanished. Kirk stood up feeling fully refreshed and whole.

McCoy was staring. Kirk nodded. "Yes. The pain is gone. Soon after she touched my head it went."

"And the wound is completely healed! What's more, it fits in, Jim. She must be an *empath!* Her nervous system is so highly responsive, so sensitive that she can actually *feel* others' emotional and physical reactions. They become part of her."

Kirk smiled at Gem. "What does one say for what you've done? My thanks."

"Captain . . ." It was Spock returning. He pointed to the left. "In that direction my tricorder picked up a substantial collection of objects—electronically sophisticated devices. I fail to understand why the tricorder gave no previous indication of anything out there."

"It's there now, Mr. Spock. Let's check it out." They were turning to leave when Kirk looked back at Gem. "Wait a minute." He went to her. "If they find you alone here, it could be dangerous. Will you come with us?"

She nodded, rising from the couch.

Because of the dimness the going was slow. They had to edge past large, contorted rock formations that reared up out of sight. Then, ahead of them, Kirk saw a glimmer of light. As they approached it, the rocks ended and the light grew brilliantly dazzling. It shone down from the ceiling of what seemed to be an enormous laboratory. An odd laboratory. All its complex instrumentation hung in midair.

They spread out to examine it. McCoy, Gem beside him, puzzled over an octagonal, bulb-studded object. Spock had gone straight to the viewing screens; but Kirk, after a cursory glance at a blank panel, was peering into blackness that lay beyond the light's reach. Suddenly glare struck him in the face. It illuminated the lab's dark corner. He backed away, disbelief and horror struggling in his face. "Spock, Bones. *Look!*"

Two large test tubes were suspended from the ceiling. Stuffed into them were the bodies of Linke and Ozaba, their features twisted with agony. The test tubes were labeled. One read "SUBJECT: LINKE." The other said, "SUBJECT: OZABA."

McCoy's voice roused Kirk from his daze. Bones was calling, "Jim! Spock!"

They crossed to him at a run. Wordless, he was pointing to three empty test tubes. The labels they bore read: "McCOY—SPOCK—KIRK."

The chord sounded hollowly in the big room. The *Enterprise* men wheeled. T-bar in hand, Lal was facing them. He eyed their shocked faces disinterestedly. "We are on schedule," he said. "But some further simple tests are necessary."

"We've just seen the results of some of your . . . tests!" McCoy shouted.

"And I have found our missing men dead." Kirk's voice shook. "Another of your experiments?"

THE EMPATH

"You are wrong," Lal said. "Their own imperfections killed them. They were not fit subjects. Come, time is short."

"*Your* time has just about run out!" Kirk cried. "This planet is about to nova. When it does, it will finish itself, you and your whole insane torture chamber along with it! As for your experiments . . ."

The three exchanged a fast glance. Kirk and McCoy strode toward the Vian. He backed away. As the two circled him, Spock closed in with his Vulcan "neck pinch." Lal collapsed. Spock removed his T-bar control. As he rose from his stoop, the bar in his hand, his tricorder beeped. Lifting it, he said, "Readings indicate passage to the surface lies in that direction, Captain." He gestured to their right.

When the party had left the lab, Lal got to his feet. Thann appeared beside him. They stood silent, their cold eyes fixed on the passageway where the group had vanished.

Spock had found his exit to the surface. Twenty minutes of clambering over rocks had brought them into the open. The red sky was overcast and the stiff wind was blowing harder. Kirk took out his communicator. "Kirk to *Enterprise*. Come in, *Enterprise!*" There was no answer. The Starship was still out of range. Belting the communicator, Kirk saw that Spock was pouring over his tricorder.

"Report, Mr. Spock?"

Spock looked up. "The research station is six kilometers from here, Captain. Straight ahead."

"Let's get there as fast as we can. If the ship has a search party looking for us, it will be there." He took Gem's hand; but a blast of wind struck her and she halted, blinded by the whip of sand in her eyes. He made to pick her up in his arms. She shook her head, smiling; and hooking her arm under his, struggled forward again. Fiercely blowing sand became a hazard to them all. Its hard grit hit McCoy's eyes so that he stumbled over a rock that tumbled him head over heels. Spock was hauling him to his feet when Gem rushed from Kirk to help McCoy. He grinned at her reassuringly. "I'm all right," he told her. "Don't worry about me, Gem."

Kirk, shading his eyes, peered ahead through the driving sand. "How much farther?" he asked Spock.

"Just ahead, sir."

McCoy gave a shout. "Jim! Look . . . Scotty and a search party!"

Before the metal hut, Scott and two Security guards were waving to them. The howl of wind drowned their voices.

"Scotty! Scotty!" Kirk yelled.

He was racing forward when he suddenly realized that Gem had fallen behind. He turned to help—and saw the Vians standing on a rock observing them.

Gem was down, her white face wet with sweat and effort. He picked her up, pushing her after Spock and McCoy. "Keep going!" he cried.

He watched her stumble on. Then, to cover the others' retreat, he ran toward the Vians.

Lal spoke to Thann. "Their will to survive is great."

"They love life greatly to struggle so."

Lal nodded. "The prime ingredient." He pointed a T-bar at the onrushing Kirk; and at once the *Enterprise* Captain felt his strength begin to ebb. Gravity became the enemy—a monstrous leech sucking, sucking at his vitality. Weaving, he reached the foot of the rock where the Vians waited—and fell.

He opened his eyes to see Spock bending over him. Fighting the fatigue that still drained his power, he sat up, crying, "What are you doing here? What happened to Scotty?"

"Mr. Scott and the guards were a mirage, Captain."

The Vians' resources seemed as infinite as their will was inexorable. He heard Thann speak his name. He looked up.

"We have decided that one specimen will be sufficient. You will come with us, Captain Kirk."

Kirk got to his feet. "And the others?"

"We have no interest in them," Lal said. "They may go."

McCoy had joined Spock. At the look of relief in

Kirk's face, he burst into protest. "You can't go back there! You'll end up like the other two!"

Spock spoke. "Captain, I request permission to be allowed to remain. . . ."

"Denied," Kirk said.

"But, Jim . . ."

"You have your orders!"

Without a backward look, Kirk started to climb the hillock topped by the rock. Spock, McCoy and Gem moved after him.

The rock was flat as a table. As Kirk walked up to the Vians, Lal said, "You are prepared?"

"Let's get on with it!" Kirk looked into the frigid Vian eyes—and a suspicion chilled him. He turned to check on the others' whereabouts. Spock and McCoy had disappeared. For a moment a hot rage choked him so that he was unable to speak. Then he said, "Where are my friends?"

"They are safe."

"Where are they? You said they'd be released! You said you needed one specimen! *One specimen!* You have it—me! Let the others go!"

Thann nodded to Lal. "Indeed the prime ingredient."

Kirk was shaking. "Never mind the ingredients! Where are my men? Tell me!" The rage broke free. He leaped at Thann. The control bar was lifted. In mid-leap Kirk winked out.

The *Enterprise* was having its troubles. The solar flares had not diminished. A worried Sulu, turning to Scott in Kirk's command chair, said, "Cosmic ray concentration is still above acceptable levels for orbiting the planet, sir."

Scott went to him. "I don't like it, Mr. Sulu. Constant exposure to this much radiation could raise the hob with Life Support and our other vital systems."

"Shall I change course to compensate, sir?"

"Not yet." Scott punched the intercom. "Bridge to all sections. We will continue to maintain our present position outside the Minarian star system. Report any sudden increase in radiation levels to the bridge immediately. Medical sections and Life Support will remain on standby alert." Swinging his chair to the helm station, he said,

"Mr. Sulu, estimate how much longer we have until those solar flares subside."

Eyeing his viewer, Sulu moved buttons on his console. "Readings now indicate 2.721 on the Van Allen scale, sir. At the present rate of decrease, we'll have to wait at least seventeen more hours before we can even attempt entering orbit."

Scott nodded glumly. "Aye. Well, as long as we're stuck out here, we might just as well relax and wait till the storm has passed."

"It has already lasted four more hours than we anticipated, sir. Do you think our landing party could be in any danger?"

"Not likely, Mr. Sulu. The planet's atmosphere will give them ample protection. If I know Captain Kirk, he's more worried about us than we are about him...."

Kirk had been stripped to the waist. His arms were stretched wide, held in their spread-eagled position by two shackles. He was drenched with sweat. Gem, clinging to a laboratory table, was trembling, her eyes closed.

"All right," he said wearily. "What is it you want to know?"

"We seek no 'information,' as you understand the word. Your civilization is yet too immature to possess knowledge of value to us," Lal said.

Kirk raised his heavy head. "Our knowledge has no value but you're willing to kill to get it! Is that what happened to Linke and Ozaba?"

Thann took a step toward him. *"We* did not kill them! Their own fears did it!"

"Just exactly what did you expect from them? What is it you want from me?"

"We have already observed the intensity of your passions, Captain. We have gauged your capacity to love others. Now we want you to reveal your courage and strength of will."

Kirk's shoulders were going numb. "Why?" he said, his head drooping. He forced it up. "Why, Lal? What do you hope to prove?" The shackles were too tight. It was their bite into the flesh of his arms that was keeping him conscious. He was glad of the shackles—but tired. Very tired. "If . . . if my death is going to have any meaning, at least tell me what I am dying for."

Lal lifted his control bar. A flicker of light played over Kirk's swaying body. At the table Gem staggered.

The Vians' transporter had conveyed Spock and McCoy back to the arena. McCoy followed Spock as the Vulcan used his tricorder. "The passage out was there before, Spock! It's got to be there now!"

"I am unable to lock in on the previous readings, Doctor. I can find no exit from here."

A circle of light flared before the couch. It widened, materializing into the forms of Kirk and Gem. His wrists were torn and bleeding; and the swollen veins on his neck were blue. When Spock and McCoy rushed to him, the force field flung them back.

"Jim! What have they done to you?"

Inside the field, Gem had taken Kirk's bleeding hands in hers. Her face and body writhed with his agony. Then red stigmata, identical to his wounds, appeared on her wrists. She backed away and the marks faded. She hesitated, looking at Spock and McCoy.

McCoy stopped straining to reach Kirk. "Help him, Gem. Don't be afraid to help him."

She kept her eyes on them as though the sight of them gave her strength. Again she took Kirk's bleeding wrists —and again her own began to bleed. But this time she ignored both her pain and her wounds. She knelt down on the floor and, cradling Kirk's head on her lap, began to massage his neck and shoulders. Once more there was the strange effect of her touch. His pain visibly eased. Their injuries vanished at the same moment. Gently she laid his head on the floor. Then she slid away from him, too weakened to get to her feet. Kirk reached out a hand to her.

The force field dissolved. Spock and McCoy hurried to them. Still dazed, Kirk struggled to rise. "Gem?" he whispered.

"Lie still!" McCoy said. "I'll check her out right now."

He had to carry her to her couch. Her eyes were closed. McCoy was staring at his medical tricorder, incredulous. The body he'd laid on the couch had been almost transparent, as though entirely drained of life. Now, before his eyes, it was recovering its solidity. Smiling, Gem looked up at McCoy. He smoothed the soft hair back from her forehead and left her to go to Kirk.

He was sitting up. "Is she all right?"

"She seems fine again."

"Bones, can you explain what happened?"

McCoy spoke excitedly. "Complete empathy—that's what it was! She must be a totally functional Empath! Her nervous system actually connected to yours to counteract the worst of your symptoms. With her strength she virtually sustained your physiological reactions."

"It weakened her," Kirk said. "I could feel it. Does this ability endanger her life?"

"It's impossible to say yet. Supplying life support to you *did* drain her."

Spock said, "She was afraid to approach the Captain after the first sharp impact of his pain. It was only your urgent plea, Doctor, that caused her to continue."

"Fear would naturally be the first reaction, Spock." McCoy went to the couch and took Gem's hands. Smiling at her, he said, "She doesn't know our Captain well enough—not yet—to offer up her life for him."

"Could the strain really have killed her?" Kirk persisted.

"I would assume that her instinct for self-preservation would take over to prevent that, Jim." He returned to Kirk. "How do you feel?"

"Tired . . . just tired."

"Captain, can you recall what happened?"

Kirk spoke slowly. "I'm not sure. I remember the laboratory . . . there was something they wanted to know. What it was I can't remember." His voice rose. "I wish I could! I can't!"

"Easy does it, Jim. Take it easy."

"What's wrong with me, Bones?"

McCoy studied his tricorder, frowning. "You have all the symptoms of the 'bends.' Nitrogen bubbles in your blood caused the pain. But how did you get the bends down here?"

"You'll have to ask the Vians." Vigor was returning to his voice. "Will I live?"

"You could still use some time in a decompression

chamber. Otherwise your recovery is just about miraculous. I wish that I could take the credit for it, but Gem did most of the work."

Spock was examining the control bar he'd taken from Thann. "Captain," he said, "I noted that a circle of light preceded you at the moment you were returned here from the Vians' laboratory."

"Spock, do you have to get so analytical? At a time like this?"

"Bones, Spock is right. Continue, Mr. Spock."

"I conclude that such a light is an energy transfer point linking this device to the power source."

"Can you tap into it?"

"If I can determine the frequency at which this device operates I could cause it to function for us."

"And get us out of here the same way they brought us here."

"I would say so, Captain."

"Then get started, Mr. Spock."

But the organ chord that invariably heralded some new Vian mischief sounded once more. The two long-robed creatures stood just outside the circle of light that still shone down before Gem's couch.

Lal addressed Kirk. "You are called 'Captain.' You are responsible for the lives of your crew. Is this correct?"

"It is correct," Kirk said.

Thann stepped forward. "We find it necessary to have the cooperation of one of your men in our efforts."

"We will not cooperate," Kirk said.

Lal continued as though he hadn't spoken. "When we resume our interrogations, you will decide which of your men we shall use. There is an 87 percent possibility that the Doctor will die. And though Commander Spock's life is in no danger, the large probability is that he will suffer brain damage resulting in permanent insanity."

They vanished.

Still weakened by his ordeals, Kirk had centered his hopes on Thann's T-bar. He crossed to where Spock was working on it to discover its operating frequency. "How's it coming, Spock?"

"I do not know, Captain. I begin to understand the principles by which it functions—but that is all."

Responsible for the lives of his crew. Lal's definition of *his* function. How to fulfill it? For Bones—probable death in that laboratory. For Spock—derangement of that exquisitely precise organ of his: his mind.

McCoy joined them. "Spock, it won't be too long before those Vians come back. You'd better find out how that thing works—and soon!"

Kirk gave his own words back to him. "Easy does it, Bones. Take it easy."

"Men weren't intended to be this far underground! It's not natural!"

"And space travel is?" Kirk asked.

Without looking up from his task, Spock said, "I must disagree, Doctor. Witness the men who pass a majority of their lives in mines beneath the surface."

"I'm a doctor, not a coalminer!"

Now Spock looked up from the T-bar. "Doctor, I have recorded my theories and procedures on the tricorder. Should the Vians return, there is sufficient data for you and the Captain to complete the adjustments."

McCoy's anxiety, exploded in irritation. "I'm no mechanic! I couldn't get that thing to work no matter how many notes you left!"

"Possibly not. But you and the Captain *together* are capable of doing so."

"In any case, you, Spock, are the *logical* choice to leave with the Captain. I am the man who should go with the Vians."

Kirk intervened. "The decision is mine! If there are any decisions to be made, *I'll* make them!" He paused. "If and when it becomes necessary."

Gem had been listening intently. Wearily Kirk sat down on the couch beside her. The combinations of mental and physical strains had exhausted his last reserves of strength. He rested his head in his hands, shutting his eyes. A hypo hissed against his shoulder. He didn't move. "What is it, Bones? I don't need any—"

"I'm still Chief Medical Officer of the *Enterprise*. Would you rather have the bends? . . . Still dizzy?"

"A little."

"Lie down until the hypo takes effect. Gem, sit beside him. Watch him."

Kirk lay down, too tired to argue. As his breathing assumed the quiet regularity of sleep, McCoy nodded his satisfaction and Spock, looking up again from the control bar, said, "How long will he be asleep?"

"Between the emotional drains and that attack of the bends, he's in pretty bad shape, Spock."

"I am not criticizing your action, Doctor. On the contrary, I am grateful for it. The Captain will not be additionally strained by making so difficult a decision. You have simplified the situation considerably."

McCoy looked at him warily. "How?"

"While the Captain is asleep, it is I who am in command. When the Vians return, I shall go with them."

The appalled McCoy looked down at his hypo. "You mean if I hadn't given him that shot . . . ?"

"Precisely. The choice would have been the Captain's. Now it is mine." He bent over the control bar, his face expressionless as ever. McCoy stared at him a moment. Then, returning to Kirk, he checked him over. Satisfied, he replaced the hypo in his medikit. Cursing under his breath, he gave Spock a savage glance. It was noted by Gem, who'd been taking in the argument. She rose now to move noiselessly until she was standing between Kirk and Spock. Kirk stirred restlessly, fighting the unconsciousness of the drug. Spock looked over at him, hesitated, then resumed his work. Gem went to him, touching his shoulder. He didn't look up. She withdrew the hand, looking at it. Then the shining eyes returned to Spock. In her face was a look of wondering love. She had seen past the coldly logical front Spock presented to the world to what the Vulcan officer kept carefully hidden—his love for his Captain and McCoy.

McCoy had seen the look on her face. His own changed abruptly as he came to a decision of his own. Apology in his eyes, he glanced at the impassive Spock, took out his hypo; and crossing to Kirk as though to check him, suddenly whirled—and injected Spock.

Spock stared at him in angry comprehension. "Your actions are highly unethical! My decision stands! I am in command and. . . ." He slumped forward.

McCoy put a hand on his shoulder. "Not this time, Spock," he said softly.

The organ notes sounded. The Vians had returned.

McCoy spoke quickly. "The choice has been made." He extended his hand back to Gem. "You stay with my friends. They will take care of you." He turned. "Do you understand, Gem?"

She looked at him. Thann, exchanging a glance with Lal, said, "Come, then."

McCoy started toward them. Then he looked back toward the sleeping Kirk and Spock. The look was a silent farewell. Tears filled Gem's eyes. They were merciful tears. They dimmed the sight of McCoy as he followed the Vians.

The shackles were stained with Kirk's blood. The Vians had not been content with McCoy's outstretched arms or the threat of his imminent death. They had placed him so as to force his eyes to the empty test tube with his name on it.

A master of the art of suspense, Lal made a speech. "Doctor, please understand that if there were any other way to accomplish our purpose, we should employ it."

McCoy could feel the veins in his neck swelling. "Get on with it!" he told them.

They advanced on him. Thann raised a control bar.

A white-faced Kirk was prowling the arena. "Spock, why . . . *why* did you let him do it?"

The composed voice said, "I was convinced in the same way you were, Captain—by the good Doctor's hypo." Spock looked up, meeting Kirk's eyes. A message flashed between them. Kirk nodded slightly to their mutual recognition of McCoy's devotion. Then a dissonant chord rang from Spock's control bar. Kirk hurried to him, asking, "Anything, Spock?"

Spock leaned back, regarding the bar with admiration. Extending it to Kirk, he said, "A most unusual device. It is a control unit but *not* a control mechanism. It is, in fact, a mechanical device."

"What exactly is it?"

"The control is attuned to only one pattern of electrical energy—the pattern produced by the mental impulses of the person who possesses it. It is activated solely through mental commands."

"Can it be adapted or . . . or reattuned to our brain patterns?"

"I am attempting to do so." Spock paused. "However, it is not possible to adjust the control for more than one pattern at a time. As I am most familiar with my own pattern, with your permission, Captain . . ."

"Do whatever you think best to get it working. What disturbs me is why the Vians have allowed it to remain in our possession."

Spock bent again over the bar. "Understandable, sir. They must know that we are capable of comprehending the control and of making use of it."

"They must know we will use it to escape."

Spock nodded. "The only logical assumption is that they wish to let us go."

"While they still have McCoy?"

"It is evidently their intention, Captain."

Kirk paced the length of the arena. Turning, he looked at Gem. Then slowly he went to her. "Somehow you are the crux . . . the focal point of all this." He wheeled to Spock. "Even before we got here, she was a prisoner. Yet they haven't hurt her. They haven't even made threats."

"Indeed, Captain, the facts indicate that she is essential to their purpose."

"Yes . . . there is purpose. *But what is it?*"

Kirk, taking Gem's hands in his, looked intently into the sensitive face, as though it held his answer. "Gem, did those who preceded us die . . . for you? Has all this . . . this pain and terror . . . happened—or been made to happen—for you?"

Spock broke into his concentration. "Completed, Captain. The adjustments are delicate. They may not survive more than one use. Even so, there should be sufficient power to return us to the *Enterprise*."

"Will it take us to McCoy?"

"If you so desire, sir."

Kirk spoke briskly. "The best defense is a strong offense. And I intend to start offending!"

The circle of light still lay before Gem's couch. Kirk stepped into it. Spock followed him. Silently, Gem joined them, McCoy's medikit in her hand. She passed it to Kirk.

He looked at her, his face drawn with anxiety. "Aim for the lab," he said to Spock.

Spock stared down at the bar he held, eyes fixed in concentration. The arena vanished. They were in the lab. Kirk looked around it. Then, stunned, he saw what he had to see.

McCoy hung limply from ropes attached to the ceiling. His features were battered to a pulp. Blood dripped from his open wounds and through the remnants of his uniform.

Kirk broke out of his shocked horror. He ran to the tortured body, supporting its weight in his arms. When Spock had removed the shackles, they carried it to a table, easing it down gently. Kirk reached for a torn wrist. "The pulse is almost gone." Spock, at the head of the table, was busy with a medical tricorder.

"Spock, what are the readings?"

"Heart, severely damaged; signs of congestion in both lungs; evidence of massive circulatory collapse."

From the corner where she huddled, Gem was watching their every move. In the harsh lab light McCoy's face was colorless, his lips faintly blue. His eyes shuddered open, stared blankly, then focused.

Kirk found water. Raising McCoy's head, he poured some into the smashed lips. "Don't try to talk, Bones." He laid the head back on the table. "Don't try to speak. Don't think. Just take it easy until we can get back to the ship. Don't—"

"Captain . . ."

Something in Spock's tone caught Kirk's alarmed attention. "What is it? What's the matter?"

With a visible effort Spock looked up from the tricorder. "Captain, I . . . he's dying. We can make him comfortable but that is all."

"No! You can't be sure, Spock! You're not a doctor."

McCoy whispered, "But . . . I am. Go on, Spock. . . ."

Spock moved the tricorder over the entire body. "Internal injuries; bleeding in chest and abdomen; hemorrhages of the spleen and liver; 70 percent kidney failure. . . ."

"He's right, Jim." McCoy grinned weakly. "Being a doctor has its drawbacks. . . . I've always wondered—" A bout of coughing silenced him. Kirk supported his head

THE EMPATH 47

until it passed. Then he tore a piece from McCoy's mangled shirt. Dipping it in the water, he dampened the hot forehead.

"Thanks... Jim...."

Kirk, his face suddenly appearing ten years older, looked at Spock. "How long?"

Spock hesitated; but at McCoy's faint nod, he said, "It could happen at any time, Captain."

The broken mouth moved in a smile. "The correct medical phrase, eh, Spock?" Coughing assailed him again, this time so violently that he seemed unable to breathe. It ceased abruptly, leaving him motionless.

"Doctor!" Spock felt for the neck pulse. He found it. Straightening, he rested his hand briefly on McCoy's head. McCoy opened his eyes, met Spock's—and their unspoken loyalty was wordlessly spoken. Then a spasm of pain twisted McCoy's face. He writhed on the table, coughing. The fit lasted so long that it suffocated him.

"Can't we do something?" Kirk said.

"I'm afraid not, Captain." As Spock spoke, McCoy lost consciousness.

Kirk said, "Gem!" They both turned toward her. "Gem could help him!" Kirk cried. "As she helped me!"

She was cowering in her corner. At the sight of her overwhelming fear, Kirk hesitated. "Could his nearness to death also kill her?"

"The Doctor's analysis of her life-support reactions assumed that the instinct for self-preservation would prevent that. However, he could not be positive."

"If she could just strengthen him to keep him from sinking further into death, we could take over, Spock, with Bones directing us."

They had started toward her when the chord suddenly reverberated at full power. The force field encircled them.

The Vians' arms were lifted in nameless threat. Lal's T-bar was extended downward. "No interference will be permitted!" he said.

Imprisoned, Kirk spoke from within the field. He was openly pleading. "She can save his life! Let us help her go to him!"

"She must neither be forced nor urged to take action."

"All must proceed without interference," Thann added.

"The purpose that brought us together—" Lal began.

"What purpose?" Kirk shouted. "What purpose can any of this serve except the satisfaction of some sick need of yours?"

"We have but one need left in life," Lal said. "It is to see the completion of the final moment of our test."

"Be patient," Thann urged.

"Patient!" Kirk's scorn was fierce with fury. "Our friend is dying!"

"Perhaps," Thann said.

"What purpose will our friend's death serve other than your pleasure in it?" Spock's voice had never been so toneless. "Surely beings as advanced as you know that your solar system will soon be extinct. This star of yours will nova."

"We know," Thann said.

"Then you know that the many millions of inhabitants on its planets are doomed."

The chill voice of Lal said, "That's why we are here."

Kirk swept the laboratory with a gesture. "This place of death you have devised for your pleasure—will it prevent that catastrophe?"

"No, it will not. That is true. But it may save Gem's planet. Of all the planets of Minara, we are empowered to transport to safety only the inhabitants of one." Thann's eyes fixed on Kirk's. "If Gem's planet is the sole one to be saved, we must make certain beyond all doubt that its people are worthy of survival."

"And how will that be served by the death of our friend?"

Lal answered. "His death will not serve it. Only Gem's willingness to give her life for him will. You were her teachers."

"Her teachers? What did she learn from us?"

"Your will to survive; your love of life; your passion to know. These qualities are recorded in her being." He paused. "Each one of you has been ready to give his life for the others. We must now find out whether that instinct has been transmitted to Gem."

The laboratory equipment rattled. The earth rumbled under the pressures of another quake. Thann spoke to Lal. "Time is growing short."

THE EMPATH

Spock looked down at McCoy's ravaged face. "You were correct, Captain. Everything that has occurred here has been caused to happen by them. This place has been a great laboratory and we have been the subjects of a test."

"No!" Thann said. "Only the circumstances were created by us. They were necessary."

Lal stepped toward Kirk. "Your actions have been spontaneous. What is truest and best in any species of beings has been revealed by you. Yours are the qualities that make a civilization worthy to survive. We are grateful to you."

"Look!" Thann cried.

Gem had left her corner. She moved to McCoy, passing through the force field as though it didn't exist. She passed her hands gently over the wounds on his face and body. Staring at her, hope returned to the *Enterprise* men.

Thann turned to Lal. "This is most significant. An instinct new to the essence of her being is generating. We are seeing it come to birth. . . ."

Lal nodded. "Compassion for another is becoming part of her functioning life system."

The fearful injuries on McCoy's face were transferring themselves to Gem's. His eyes fluttered open, their pupils still glazed. Tensely, Kirk watched for some body movement. It didn't come. But the wounds on his face had begun to heal; and those on Gem's were disappearing. McCoy moved his head. Looking at Gem, recognition replaced the glaze in his eyes.

She was growing weak. Fear came into her great eyes. She withdrew from the table and staggered back toward her corner. McCoy's wounds began to bleed again.

"She is saving herself," Lal said. "She does not yet possess the instinct to save her people."

"We have failed," Thann said.

Spock spoke to Kirk. "Captain, the Doctor's life is not solely dependent on Gem. The Vians also must have the power to give him back his life."

Lal addressed Spock directly. "Your friend's death is not important. We must wait to see whether her instinct for self-sacrifice has become stronger than her instinct for self-preservation."

Watching, Kirk could see signs of the anguished internal struggle in the girl. Then her white face cleared with decision. She returned to McCoy, her step firm and determined. Kneeling beside the table, she took his limp hands in hers. Again, his wrists' gashes transferred to hers. McCoy's body moved—but life once again seemed to be draining from her.

McCoy lifted his head. "Don't touch me," he told her. "Stay away."

He tried to look around. "Jim . . . Spock . . . are you here?"

"Yes, Bones."

"Don't let her touch me. She will die."

He hauled himself to his knees, struggling to pull his hands from Gem's. The effort exhausted him. He fell back, looking pleadingly at Kirk. "Make her leave me . . . Jim . . . Spock. . . . I will not destroy life. Not even to save my own. You know that. Please . . . make her leave me."

Gem placed her hand on his heart. Color, faint but visible, came into McCoy's face.

"Captain!"

"Yes, Spock."

"The intensity of emotion that is exhausting us is building up the force field around us!"

"I know. It draws its energy from us."

"In spite of what we see, sir, all emotions must be eliminated. This may weaken the field."

"I'll try, Spock."

Both closed their eyes. A complete calm was in Spock's face. Even concentration was absorbed by his serenity. His hand went through the force field. He moved through it and quietly approached the Vians. Still held by the field, Kirk tried to still his tumult of anxieties. He looked at the Vians. They were so tense with their will to power that they failed to note Spock's position behind them. The Vulcan's arm rose; and lashed down in a judo chop that sent Lal's T-bar flying. The force field broke. As Kirk raced out of it, Spock retrieved the T-bar. Physically helpless now, the Vians hesitated, their essential test threatened with final disaster.

Gem was swaying with increasing weakness. McCoy dragged himself to his knees, crying, "No! No! I won't let you do it!" He shoved her away in a momentary influx of strength. Frightened by his sudden violence, she shrank from the table. As McCoy tried to move further away from her, his wounds reopened. He fell back, lying still. Gem stumbled back to her corner.

Kirk took the T-bar from Spock. He was rushing to McCoy with it when Lal spoke. "You cannot use our powers to change what is happening."

Kirk looked at the deathly white face on the table Then he went to the Vians. "You must save the life of our friend."

"No. We will not," Lal said. "Her instinct must develop to the full. The test must be complete."

"It *is* complete." Spock joined Kirk. "Gem has already earned the right of survival for her planet. She has offered her life."

"To offer is insufficient proof," Lal said.

"If death is the only proof you can understand, then here are four lives for you." Kirk proffered the T-bar to Lal.

The Vian stared at him. "We will not leave our friend," Kirk said.

Lal took the bar. Turning, the two *Enterprise* officers strode back to McCoy.

At the table, Kirk faced around. "You are frauds," he said. "You have lost the capacity to feel the very emotions you brought Gem here to experience! You don't know the meaning of life. Compassionate love is dead in you! All you are is arid intellect!"

Lal's face went rigid with shock. Thann began to tremble. Their very bodies seemed to dwindle as Kirk's words struck home. They looked at each other, lost, the values of their lifetime dissolving. Lal was the first to move. Thann followed him to the table. They stood there a long moment, looking down at McCoy. Then Lal passed the T-bar over him. McCoy sat up, whole.

Nobody spoke. The Vians went to Gem. They lifted her in their arms. With her head on his shoulder, Lal turned, the first glint of warmth in his aged face. "The one emotion left to us is gratitude," he said. "We are thankful that we can express it to you. Farewell."

They chose to vanish slowly, changing into mist. Gem,

looking back at the *Enterprise* trio, was the last to disappear.

The bridge viewing screen held the images of the immortal stars. Kirk turned away from it. Among them was a mortal star about to die.

"Strange..." he said.

Beside him, Spock said, "What puzzles you, Captain?"

"Puzzled isn't the word, Mr. Spock. I think I am awed."

"I'm with you, Jim," McCoy said. "She awed me."

"I wasn't thinking of Gem," Kirk said. He looked back at the viewing screen. "I was thinking of the fantastic element of chance that out in limitless space we should have come together with the savior of a planet."

Spock said, "The element of chance, Captain, can virtually be eliminated by a civilization as advanced as the Vians'."

Scott spoke from his station. "Not to dispute your computer, Mr. Spock—but from the little you have told me, I would say she was a pearl of great price."

"What, Scotty?"

"You know the story of the merchant . . . that merchant 'who when he found one pearl of great price, went and sold all he had and bought it.'"

"She was that all right, Scotty," Kirk said. "And whether the Vians bought her or found her, I am glad for her and the planet she will save."

"Personally," McCoy said, "I find it *fascinating* that with all their scientific knowledge and advances, it was good old-fashioned *human emotion* they valued the most."

"Perhaps the Vulcans should hear about this," said Scott.

"Mr. Spock, could you be prevailed upon to give them the news?"

Spock looked at them blandly. "Possibly, Captain. I shall certainly give the thought its due consideration."

"I am sure you will, Mr. Spock." Kirk turned to Sulu. "Helmsman, take us out of orbit. Warp factor two."

At high speed the *Enterprise* left the area of the dying star.

THE GALILEO SEVEN

(Simon Wincelberg & Oliver Crawford)

The USS *Enterprise* operated under a standing order to investigate all quasar and quasarlike phenomena wherever and whenever it encountered them. To Kirk, it seemed to have met up with one. A sinister formation had appeared on the bridge's main viewing screen—a bluish mass, threaded with red streaks of radiant energy. It dominated the sky ahead.

Kirk, eyeing the screen, pushed a button, only too conscious of the critical presence of his passenger, High Commissioner Ferris. "Captain to shuttlecraft *Galileo*," he said. "Stand by, Mr. Spock."

Ferris voiced his disapproval. "I remind you, Captain, that I am entirely opposed to this delay. Your mission is to get those medical supplies to Makus III in time for their transfer to the New Paris colonies."

"And I must remind you of our standing order, sir. There will be no problem. It's only three days to Makus III. And the transfer doesn't take place for five."

Ferris was fretful. "I don't like to take chances. With the plague out of control on New Paris, we must get those drugs there in time."

"We will." Kirk turned back to his console. "Captain to *Galileo*. All systems clear for your take-off."

"Power up, Captain. All instruments activated. All readings normal. All go."

Spock's voice . . . reassuring. As Science Officer, he was commanding the investigating team selected from the *Enterprise* crew for research into the space curiosity charted under the name of Murasaki 312. Now he sat, strapped, in the shuttlecraft's pilot seat, the others behind him—McCoy, Scott, Yeoman Mears, a fresh-faced girl, Boma, the Negro astrophysicist, radiation specialist Gaetano, navigator Latimer. All together, seven: the *Galileo*'s seven.

"Launch shuttlecraft," Kirk said.

On the huge flight deck the heavy hangar doors swung open. The shuttlecraft taxied toward them and moved out into the emptiness of space.

Spock spoke over his shoulder. "Position."

"Three point seven . . . no, no, sir," Latimer said. "Four point—"

"Make up your mind," Spock said.

"My indicator's gone crazy," Latimer said.

Boma spoke quickly. "To be expected, Mr. Spock. Quasars are extremely disruptive. Just how much, we don't know. . . ."

Spock, eyes on his panel, said dryly, "Considerably, Mr. Boma."

Gaetano made his discouraging contribution. "My radiation reading is increasing rapidly, Mr. Spock!"

"Stop forward momentum!"

Latimer pushed switches. "I can't stop it, sir! Nothing happens!" McCoy leaned over to glance at his instruments. "Spock, we're being drawn right into the thing!"

Struggling with his own controls, Spock said, "Full power astern!"

But there was no power to reverse the onward plunge of the *Galileo*. "What's happening?" McCoy cried.

Boma said, "We underestimated the strength of the nucleonic attraction."

Spock reached for his speaker. *"Galileo* to *Enterprise.* We're out of control, Captain! Being pulled directly into the heart of Murasaki 312. Receiving violent radiation on outer. . . ."

A blast of static drowned Spock's voice. Kirk rushed over to Uhura's station. "Can't you get anything at all, Lieutenant?"

"Nothing clear, sir. Not on any frequency. Just those couple of words about being pulled off course."

Kirk wheeled. "Mr. Sulu, get me a fix on the *Galileo!*"

Sulu turned a bewildered face. "Our scanners are blocked, Captain. We're getting a mess of readings I've never seen before. Nothing makes sense!"

Kirk strode to the library computer. He got a hum, a click—and the flat, metallic computer voice. "Negative ionic concentration 1.64 by 10^2 meter. Radiation wavelength 370 angstroms, harmonics upwards along entire spectrum."

Kirk turned, appalled. Staring at him, Ferris said, "What is it, Captain?"

"That thing out there has completely ionized this entire sector!"

He glared at the screen. "At least four complete solar systems in this vicinity—and somewhere out there is a twenty-four-foot shuttlecraft out of control, off its course. Finding a needle in a haystack would be child's play compared to finding . . ."

Coiling, hungry, the bluish mass on the screen glared back at him, a blight on the face of space.

But the controls of the shuttlecraft weren't the only victims of Murasaki 312. It had rendered useless the normal searching systems of the *Enterprise*. Without them, the Starship was drifting, blind, almost as helpless as the *Galileo*.

Ferris could not resist his I-told-you-so compulsion. "I was opposed to this from the beginning," he said to Kirk. "Our flight to Makus III had the very highest priority."

Kirk, his mind straining to contingencies that confronted the *Galileo*'s crew of seven, said, "I am aware of that, Commissioner. At the same time I have certain scientific duties—and exploring the Murasaki Effect is one of them."

"But you have lost your crew," Ferris said.

If there were people who couldn't resist an "I told you so," there were just as many who enjoyed making the painfully obvious more painful. Kirk held on to his temper. "We have two days to find them," he said.

Ferris pointed to the screen. "In all that? Two days?"

Kirk lost his temper. "Are you suggesting that I just turn around and leave them in it?"

"You shouldn't have sent them out in the first place!" Ferris paused. "You are concerned with only seven people. I am thinking of the millions in the New Paris colonies who will die if we don't get these medicines to them. It's your obstinate insistence on carrying out these inconsequential investigations that...."

A bureaucrat is a bureaucrat is a bureaucrat, Kirk thought. They could function with paper. But remove them from paper into the sphere of decisive action and they turned into moralizing futilities. Scorn restored his composure. "We will make our scheduled rendezvous, Commissioner," he said evenly. "You have my word."

Uhura spoke. "Captain, there is one planet in this vicinity capable of sustaining human life. Type M, oxygen-nitrogen. Listed as Taurus II." The sympathy in her voice was cool water to a thirsty man. Kirk went to her. She looked up at him. "It is very nearly dead center of the Murasaki Effect, as closely as we can make out with our equipment malfunctions."

"Thank you, Lieutenant," Kirk said. "Mr. Sulu?"

"Yes, sir?"

"Set course for Taurus II."

"Course laid in, sir."

"Aren't you shooting in the dark?" Ferris said. "Assuming that they are there?"

"If they aren't there, Commissioner, they are all dead by now. We will search Taurus II because there is no sense in searching any place else."

"You said something about a needle in a haystack. Useless."

"Not if you want your needle back."

Strangely enough, the needle had fallen upon soft hay. However, soft was the best you could say about the spongily ugly surface of Taurus II. It had cushioned the impact of the *Galileo*'s crash landing in a roughly circular crater. Rock walls reared up toward a sky of a repellently bilious shade of green. It was not a prepossessing planet. The craft, canted over, had banged people and things around inside. Spock was bleeding green from a cut on his head. McCoy attended to it and then made his way to Yeoman Mears.

"Are you all right?"

"I ... think so, Doctor."

Boma said, "That is what I call a ride."

"What happened?" Latimer asked him.

"I can't be sure . . . but I'd say that the magnetic potential of the Murasaki Effect was such that it was multiplied geometrically as we gathered speed. We were simply shot into the center of the Effect like a projectile. What do you think, Mr. Spock?"

"Your evaluation seems reasonable."

Scott, holding an aching head, joined Spock in checking the instruments and control panel. "What a mess!" he said.

Spock stood up. "Picturesque descriptions won't mend broken circuits, Mr. Scott. I think you'll find your work cut out for you." He threw a switch on the communicator.

"Galileo to *Enterprise.* Do you read me?"

"You don't really expect an answer, do you?" Scott said.

"I expect nothing. It is simply logical to try every alternative. A reading on the atmosphere, please, Doctor McCoy."

"As soon as I finish checking the crew . . ."

"If anyone had been injured, I assume you would have been so informed by now. The reading, Doctor."

There was irritation in the glance Spock received from McCoy. After a moment the Medical Officer picked up his kit and moved to an instrument panel. "Partial pressure of oxygen is 70 millimeters of mercury. Nitrogen, 140. Breathable, if you're not running in competition."

"The facts, please," Spock said.

"Traces of argon, neon, krypton, all in acceptable quantities. But I wouldn't recommend this place for a summer resort."

"Your opinion will be noted. You are recording this, Yeoman?"

"Of course, Mr. Spock."

"Very good. Mr. Scott, if you will immediately conduct a damage survey."

Scott said, "Naturally."

Spock ignored the tone of the comment. He said, "I suggest we move outside to give Mr. Scott room to work. Mr. Latimer, Mr. Gaetano, please arm yourselves and scout out the immediate area. Stay in visual contact with the ship."

"Aye, aye, sir," Gaetano said.

The two were removing phaser pistols from a locker as McCoy turned to Spock. "What do you think our chances are of communicating with the *Enterprise?*"

"Under current conditions, extremely poor."

"But they'll be looking for us!"

"If the ionization effect is as widespread as I believe it is, they'll be looking for us without instruments. By visual contact only. On those terms, it is a very large solar system."

"Then you don't think they'll find us."

"Not so long as we are grounded."

McCoy exploded. "I've never been able to stand your confoundedly eternal cheerfulness, Spock!"

"Better make an effort to, Doctor." The suggestion was mildly made. "We may be here for a long time."

Kirk himself had small cause for cheer. The *Enterprise* scanners had gone completely on strike. "Mr. Sulu, have you tried tying in with the auxiliary power units?"

"Yes, sir. No change."

Scowling, Kirk hit a button. "Transporter Room. This is the Captain. Are the Transporters beaming yet?"

The technician sounded apologetic. "Not one hundred percent, sir. We beamed down some inert material but it came back in a dissociated condition. We wouldn't dare try it with people."

"Thank you." He pushed another button. "Captain to Flight Deck. Prepare shuttlecraft *Columbus* for immediate search of planet surface. Correlate coordinates with Mr. Sulu. Lieutenant Uhura?"

"Yes, sir?"

"Anything at all?"

"All wavelengths dominated by ionization effect, Captain. Transmissions blocked, reception impossible."

To add to his joy in life, Ferris appeared beside Kirk's command chair. "Well, Captain?"

Kirk said, "We have until 2823.8 to continue our search, Commissioner."

"You don't really think you'll have any luck, do you?"

Kirk drew a hand down his cheek. "Those people out there happen to be friends and shipmates of mine. I intend to continue this ship's search for them until the last possible moment."

"Very well, Captain. But not a second beyond that limit. Is that clear? If it is not, I refer you to Book 19, Section 433, Paragraph 12."

"I am familiar with the regulations, Commissioner. And I know all about your authority."

Tight-faced, he struck a button on his console.

"Launch shuttlecraft *Columbus!*"

Outside the *Galileo,* Spock was examining the nearest section of the wall encircling the crater. Rescue was indeed a remote possibility. Even if the *Enterprise*'s searching equipment had remained unaffected by Murasaki 312, Taurus II was just one planet among many in the quadrant's solar systems. Hidden like this in the hollow made by the crater's rocky wall, the *Galileo* would be virtually invisible.

McCoy, joining him, looked up at the wall. "I can't say much for our circumstances," he said, "but at least it's your big chance."

"My big chance for what, Doctor?"

"Command," McCoy said. "I know you, Spock. You've never voiced it, but you've always thought logic was the best basis on which to build command. Am I right?"

"I am a logical man," Spock said.

"It'll take more than logic to get us out of this."

"Perhaps, Doctor . . . but I can't think of a better place to start trying. I recognize that command has fascinations, even under such circumstances as these. But I neither enjoy the idea of command nor am I frightened by it. It simply exists. And I shall do what logically needs to be done."

They clambered back into the craft, and Scott lifted a grim face from the control panel. "We've lost a great deal of fuel, Mr. Spock. We have no chance at all to reach escape velocity. And even if we hope to make orbit, we'll have to lighten our load by at least five hundred pounds."

"The weight of three grown men," Spock said.

Scott glanced at him, startled. "Why, yes . . . I guess you could put it that way."

McCoy was openly outraged. "Or the equivalent weight in *equipment,*" he said.

Spock faced him. "Doctor McCoy, with few exceptions we will use virtually every piece of equipment in attaining orbit. There is very little surplus weight except among our passengers."

Boma, with Yeoman Mears, had been taking tricorder readings near the hatch. Now he stopped. "You mean three of us will have to stay behind?"

"Unless the situation changes radically," Spock said.

"And who is to choose those who remain behind?"

"As commanding officer the choice is mine."

Boma's face hardened. "You wouldn't be interested in drawing lots?"

Spock said "I believe I am better qualified to select those who will stay behind than any random drawing of lots." He spoke without a trace of egotism in voice or manner. "My decision will be a logical one, Mr. Boma, arrived at through logical processes."

"Life and death are not logical, Spock!" McCoy cried.

"But attaining a desired goal is."

Spock ignored the tension in the atmosphere. "I would suggest we proceed to a more careful examination of the hull. We may have overlooked some minor damage."

Boma glared after him as he left. "Some minor damage was overlooked," he said, "when they put his head together!"

"Not his head," McCoy said. "His heart."

Tension was rising in everybody. Over at the farther crater wall Latimer and Gaetano were making a nervous survey of the area. Suddenly Gaetano stopped, listening. Latimer, too, halted. They listened to the sound—a rhythmic scraping noise such as might be made by rubbing wood against some corrugated surface. Latimer became conscious of an uneasy impression that the crater wall was breathing, the mist of its breath the fog that drifted over it, reducing visibility. The mist had come suddenly, like the sound. The scraping noise was repeated.

"What is it?" Latimer whispered.

"I don't know," Gaetano said. "It came from up there."

"No . . . back there. . . ."

They stared at each other. The sound surrounded them.

"Everywhere . . . it's all around us."

"Let's get out of here!" Latimer cried.

Then he yelled, breaking into a run. From the shadow made by a cleft in the wall above them a gigantic shape had emerged. Latimer screamed—and fell. Gaetano jerked out his phaser. He fired it at the fog-filled cleft.

He turned. The shaft of a spear was protruding from Latimer's back. It was as thick as a slim telephone pole.

The scream, reverberating against the crater's walls, had been heard by Spock and Boma. The Vulcan strode to Gaetano, where he stood over Latimer's body, still in shock, still staring up at the foggy cleft.

"How?" Spock said.

The dazed Gaetano lowered his phaser. "Something . . . huge . . . terrible. Up there!" He pointed to the cleft.

Spock walked over to the wall. Seizing an outcropping of rock, he began to climb up to the crevice. Boma spoke to Gaetano. "What was it? Did you see what it was?"

"Like a . . . a giant ape." He started to tremble. "It was all . . . so quick. There was a . . . a sound first."

Spock was back. "There's nothing up there," he said.

"I tell you there was!" Gaetano shouted.

Spock's voice was quiet. "I do not doubt your word."

"I hit it. I swear my phaser hit it," Gaetano said.

Spock didn't answer. Looking down at Latimer's body, he tugged at the spear shaft. It came loose in his hand, exposing its point—a large triangular stone, honed into shape and sharpness.

"The Folsom Point," Spock said.

"Sir?"

"Mr. Boma, this spearhead bears a remarkable resemblance to the Folsom Point, discovered in 1926 old Earth calendar, in New Mexico, North America. Quite similar . . . more crudely shaped about the haft, however. Not very efficient."

"Not very efficient?" Boma was furious. "Is that all you have to say?"

Surprised, Spock looked at him. "Am I in error, Mr. Boma?"

"Error? You? Impossible!"

"Then, what—" Spock began.

"A man lies there dead! And you talk about stone

spears! What about Latimer? What about the dead man?"

"A few words on behalf of the dead will not bring them back to life, Mr. Boma."

Gaetano was glaring at him, too. He spoke to Boma. "Give me a hand with Latimer, will you?" He turned to Spock. "Unless you think we should leave his body here in the interest of efficiency."

"Bringing him back to the ship should not interfere with our repair efforts. If you'd like some assistance . . ."

"We'll do it!" Gaetano said sharply. Nodding to Boma, they reached down to the body. As they lifted it, Spock's keen eyes were studying the spearhead's construction.

Kirk was trying to fight off a sense of complete futility.

". . . and great loss." His voice was so broken as he dictated the last three words into his Captain's Log that he wondered if he should delete them. Spock . . . McCoy . . . Scott . . . all three of them gone, lost to the hideous blueness of what still showed on the screen.

Uhura spoke. "Captain, the *Columbus* has returned from searching quadrants 779X by 534M. Negative results."

"Have them proceed to the next quadrants. Any word from Engineering on the sensors?"

"They're working on them, sir. Still inoperable."

"The Transporters?"

"Still reported unsafe, sir."

"Thank you, Lieutenant."

"Captain Kirk . . ."

It was Ferris. "Captain, I do not relish the thought of abandoning your crewmen out there. However, I must remind you that—"

"I haven't forgotten," Kirk said wearily.

"You're running out of time," Ferris said.

A man of paper. "I haven't forgotten that, either," Kirk said. He rammed a button on his console. "This is the Captain. Try using overload power on the Transporters. We have to get it working." He got up to go to Uhura. "Lieutenant, order the *Columbus* to open its course two degrees on each lap from now on."

Sulu, surprised into protest, spoke. "But Captain, two

degrees means they'll overlook more than a dozen terrestrial miles on each search loop."

Kirk turned. "It also means we'll at least have a fighting chance of checking most of the planet's surface. Mind your helm, Mr. Sulu."

Sulu flushed. "Yes, sir."

Ferris was still standing beside his command chair. He said coldly, "Twenty-four more hours, Captain."

Kirk didn't answer. He stared ahead at the viewing screen. Somewhere in the midst of that mysterious blueness, Taurus II existed, its substance solid, its air breathable—an oasis in the center of hell. Had Spock found it?

In the marooned *Galileo,* McCoy and Yeoman Mears had collected equipment to jettison. Arms laden, McCoy said, "This stuff ought to save us at least fifty pounds of weight, Spock."

"If we could scrape up another hundred pounds, what with Mr. Latimer gone . . ." Yeoman Mears didn't finish her sentence.

"We would still be at least one hundred and fifty pounds overweight," Spock said.

"I can't believe you're serious about leaving someone behind," McCoy said. "Whatever those creatures are out there . . ."

"It is more rational to sacrifice one man than six," Spock said.

"I'm not talking about rationality!"

"You might be wise to start."

Boma stuck his head through the open hatch. "We're ready, Mr. Spock."

"For what, Mr. Boma?"

"The services . . . for Latimer."

Spock straightened. "Mr. Boma. We are working against time."

"The man is dead. He deserves a decent burial. You're the Captain. A few words from you . . ."

If Spock's facial muscles had been capable of expressing annoyance, they would have twisted with it. As they were not, he looked at McCoy. "Doctor, perhaps you know the correct words for such an occasion."

"It's your place," McCoy said.

"My place is here. If you please, Doctor."

The facial muscles of the non-Vulcans had no trouble in showing annoyance. Spock's cool detachment exceedingly irritated them. "Spock, we may all die here!" McCoy shouted. "At least let us die like men, not machines!"

"By taking care of first things first, I hope to increase our chances of not dying here." Spock moved to where Scott was still at work on the console. "Perhaps if you were to channel the second auxiliary tank through the primary intake valve, Mr. Scott."

"Too delicate, sir. It may not take the pressure as it is."

McCoy glared at Spock's stooped back. Then he followed the others out of the hatch and over to the mound of earth a few feet away from the *Galileo*. He bent for a handful of dirt and dropped it on the mound. "Dust thou art and to dust shalt thou return. Amen."

People's heads bowed. "Amen," they echoed. They all stood still for a minute, each with his private thoughts— and the rhythmic grating sound came from what seemed to be distance.

"What is it?" said Yeoman Mears.

McCoy had looked up. "I don't know. But it sounds manmade."

"*Man*made! You wouldn't say that if you saw what I saw!" cried Gaetano. "It's them, those things out there somewhere!"

McCoy spoke to him and Boma. "You'd better stay on watch. I'll check with Mr. Spock."

He and Yeoman Mears re-entered the craft to hear a dismayed Scott cry, "The pressure's dropping, sir. We're losing everything!"

"What happened?" Spock asked.

"One of the lines gave. The strain of coming through the atmosphere . . . the added load when we tried to bypass—"

McCoy interrupted. "Spock!"

The Vulcan made a gesture for silence, concentrating on Scott. Staring at a gauge, the engineer said slowly, "Well, that does it. We have no fuel at all!"

"Then that solves the problem of who to leave behind."

"Spock!" McCoy yelled.

"Yes, Doctor?"

"Come outside. Something's happening."

Straightening, Spock said, "You will consider the alternatives, Mr. Scott."

Scott rose impatiently. "What alternatives? We have no fuel!"

"Mr. Scott, there are always alternatives."

He took his Vulcan calm with him as he followed McCoy out of the ship. The grating noise was louder. Spock listened, as concentrated on it as he'd been on Scott. McCoy glanced at his composed face. "And what do those super-sensitive ears of yours make of *that?*"

"Wood," Spock said. "Rubbing on some kind of leather."

"They're getting ready," Gaetano muttered. "They'll attack."

"Not necessarily," Boma said. "It could be a simple tribal rite . . . assuming it's a tribal culture."

"Not a tribal culture," Spock said gently. "Their artifacts are too primitive. Merely a loose association of some sort."

"We do not know that they are mere animals. They may well be capable of reason."

"We know they're capable of killing," Boma reminded him.

Spock looked at him. "If they are protecting themselves by their own lights . . ."

"That is exactly what we would be doing!" Boma argued.

Gaetano said, "The majority of us—"

"I am not interested in the opinion of the majority, Mr. Gaetano!" It was the first time Spock had raised his voice. Now its unexpected sharpness came as a shock to all of them.

"The components must be weighed—our dangers balanced against our duty to other life forms, friendly or not." Spock paused. "There is a third course."

"It could get us all killed." But the insolence had left Gaetano.

"I think not," Spock said. "Doctor McCoy, you and

Yeoman Mears will remain in the ship. Assist Mr. Scott in any way possible. We shall return shortly."

He turned to Gaetano and Boma. "You will follow my orders to the letter. You will fire only when so ordered— and at my designated targets."

"Now you're talking," said Gaetano.

"Yes, I am talking, Mr. Gaetano. And you will hear. We shall fire to frighten. Not to kill."

"If we only knew more about them," Yeoman Mears said fearfully.

"We know enough," Boma said. "If they're tribal, they'll have a sense of unity. We can use that."

"How, Mr. Boma?"

"By hitting them hard, sir. Give them a bloody nose! Make them think twice about attacking us! A good offense is the best defense!"

"I agree!" cried Gaetano. "If we just stand by and do nothing, we're just giving them an invitation to come down and slaughter us!"

Spock's face had taken on a look of grave reflection. "I am frequently appalled," he said, "by the low regard for life you Earth people have."

"We are practical about it!" Gaetano's voice shook. "I say we hit them before they hit us!"

"Mr. Boma?" Spock said.

"Absolutely."

"Doctor McCoy?"

"It seems logical to me."

"It also seems logical to me," Spock said. "But taking life indiscriminately . . ."

"You were quick enough to talk about leaving three of us behind," Gaetano said. "Why all the sudden solicitude about some kind of animal?"

"You saw what they did to Latimer," Boma said.

So it had to be put into words of one syllable. But Spock was a master of primitives' languages. "I am in command here, Mr. Gaetano. The orders are mine to give, as the responsibility is mine to take. Follow me."

He led the way to the crater wall. The grating sound grew still louder as the trip began the climb up the rocky escarpment. Gaetano, apprehensive, arranged himself third in position. Spock signaled a halt. The slope ahead of them loomed vague and indistinct through mist swirls. Suddenly, among the rocks immediately above them, there was movement. Spock heard it first. He tensed with alertness, readying his phaser. Something rose from behind the rocks, something impossibly huge. It might have been man-shaped—but he couldn't tell, for the creature held an enormous leather shield before its body. Then a great spear whistled past his head. Spock, aiming his phaser, fired it.

There was a roar, half-human—a scream of pain and fear. The thing ducked behind a rock, hurling its shield downward.

Spock sidestepped to avoid its strike. He was hoisiting it up as Boma and Gaetano joined him.

Awed, Gaetano whispered, "It must be twelve feet high."

Spock dropped the shield. Still leading the way, he motioned the others forward. They made the crest of the crater. Now the scraping noise was louder still, harsh, rasping, broken by grunting sounds.

"The mists . . ." Gaetano complained. "I can't see."

"They are directly ahead of us," Spock said. "Several, I believe. You will direct your phasers to two o'clock and to ten o'clock."

"I say we hit them dead on!" Gaetano said.

Spock turned his head. "Fortunately, I am giving the orders, Mr. Gaetano. Take aim, please."

He waited. "Fire!" he said.

Whatever their targets were, they could certainly howl. Spock listened to the roaring. "Cease fire!" he said. The roaring stilled. Spock nodded, satisfied. "They should think twice before bothering us again."

"I still say we should have killed them."

"It was not necessary, Mr. Gaetano. Fear will do for us what needs to be done. Mr. Boma, return to the ship. Mr. Gaetano, you will remain here on guard, keeping visual contact with the ship."

"Out here? Alone?"

"Security must be maintained, Mr. Gaetano."

Boma said, "At least let me stay with him."

"My intention is to post you in another position, Mr. Boma."

The two exchanged terrified looks. Spock regarded them with a mild curiosity. "Gentlemen," he said, "I regret having to post you in hazardous positions. Unfortunately, I have no choice. In the event of danger, the ship must have warning."

"Even if some of us must die for it?"

"There is the possibility of danger, Mr. Boma. But it cannot be helped."

He began the climb back down to the ship. After a long moment, Boma turned to follow him. "Good luck, Gaetano," he said.

"Yeah, sure," Gaetano said.

As they approached the *Galileo*, Spock said, "Mr. Boma, your post is here, near the ship." He hoisted himself through the hatch and Yeoman Mears said, "Did you find them, Mr. Spock?"

"We found them. I don't think they'll trouble us again."

"I hope not," McCoy said. "Spock, Scott has some idea."

He clearly did. Scott's face was alight with idea. "It's dangerous, Mr. Spock—but it just may work."

"Go ahead, Mr. Scott."

"I can adjust the main reactor to function on a substitute fuel supply." He paused, unable to resist the temptation to give full dramatic value to his idea. "Our phasers, sir. I could adapt them and use their energy. It will take time, but it's possible."

"The objection is they're our only defense," McCoy said.

"They would also seem to be our only hope." Spock made his decision fast. "Doctor . . . Yeoman . . . your phasers, please."

"But what if those creatures attack again?" the girl asked.

"They will not attack, not for many hours at any rate," Spock told her. "By then, with luck, we should be gone."

Scott nodded. "If I can get a full load, we'll be able to achieve orbit with all hands. Not that we can maintain it long."

"It will not be necessary to maintain it long. In less than twenty-four hours the *Enterprise* will be forced to abandon its search in order to make its rendezvous. If our orbit decays after that time, it will make no difference." Spock shrugged. "Whether we die coming out of orbit or here on the surface, we shall surely die. Your phaser, Doctor."

Reluctantly McCoy and the girl surrendered their phasers. Spock passed them over to Scott.

At the same moment on the *Enterprise*, the Transporter officer was reporting a successful materialization to Kirk. "The crates I beamed down to Taurus II came back all right, sir. In my opinion the Transporters are now safe for human transport."

It was the first good news since they had contacted Murasaki 312. Kirk pushed his intercom button. "This is the Captain. Landing parties 1, 2, and 3. Report to Transporter Room for immediate beam-down to the planet's surface. Ordinance condition 1-A."

"Captain . . . it's a big planet," the Transporter officer said. "It'll be sheer good luck if our landing parties find anything."

"I'm counting on luck, Lieutenant. It's almost the only tool we've got that might work."

But Spock, despite his hope that fear would restrain the hostility of the gorillalike creatures, wasn't trusting to luck. For the third time he left the *Galileo* to check with Boma. "Have you seen or heard anything unusual, Mr. Boma?"

"Nothing, sir."

"Is Mr. Gaetano keeping in contact with you?"

"I saw him up in those rocks just a few minutes ago."

Something else had seen Gaetano among the rocks. It aimed a large rock at his phaser, knocking it out of his hand. Terrified, he scrambled after it—and a spear hurled past him, striking the air between him and the weapon. He ran toward a rock crevice. It ended in a blank black wall. Trapped, he turned. The crevice entrance was blocked by a massive bulk, hairy, featureless. The creature moved toward him. He screamed.

It was Spock who found the dropped phaser. As he bent to retrieve it, he heard a snuffling, half-growl, half-grunt from somewhere in the rocks ahead of him. Then there was silence. McCoy and Boma climbed up to him. He extended his hand. "Mr. Gaetano's phaser," he said.

"Look!" Boma cried.

The footprint in the rubble was human in form. Its enormity was its horror.

Boma and McCoy stared at it, unbelieving. Spock handed Gaetano's phaser to McCoy. "Take this back to Mr. Scott for conversion, please, Doctor."

Boma flared up at him. "Is that all this means to you? Just a phaser to be recovered?"

Spock stared at him, puzzled. "Explain, Mr. Boma."

The frenzied Boma broke into a shout. "Gaetano's gone! Who knows what's happened to him! And you just hand over his phaser as though nothing had happened at all!"

Spock ignored the outburst. Drawing out his own phaser, he handed it over to McCoy, saying, "And please give this to Mr. Scott in case I don't return."

"Where are you going?" McCoy demanded.

Spock said, "I have a certain . . . scientific curiosity about what has occurred to Mr. Gaetano. You will return to the ship, if you please."

He slipped off into the mist, leaving Boma to gape after him. McCoy, shaking his head, said, "He'll risk his neck locating Gaetano. And if he finds him alive, he's just as liable to order him to stay behind when the ship leaves. You tell me."

"Do you think the ship will ever leave?"

"It won't without these phasers," McCoy said. "Let's get back to Scott."

Sharp-eyed, agile as a cat, Spock was creeping upward over rocks. Then he saw the ledge. Gaetano lay sprawled on it, unmoving. Spock bent over the body. As he realized what had been done to it, his impassive face went stony with revulsion. After a moment, he lifted it, hoisting it up and around his shoulders. The snuffling sound came again, this time from the mist-drifted rocks behind him. He looked back. Just the rocks, the fog coiling around them. He moved on—and suddenly the scraping noise broke out, close by, all around him, moving with him as he moved. Aware of it, he didn't hurry, but maintained his pace, measured, controlled. Below him now he could see the *Galileo,* its terrified people huddled together at the hatch, watching him.

He reached them just as a spear clanged harmlessly against the ship's hull. McCoy and Boma ran to him to help him enter the hatch. Inside, McCoy reached toward the body's lolling head. "Is he . . . ?"

"Mr. Boma, secure that hatch!" Spock said. He walked swiftly toward the aft compartment. McCoy followed him and eased the body from his shoulders. Boma, up forward near the hatch window, called, "I see one out there!" Yeoman Mears, joining him, peered out the window. Shuddering, she covered her face with her hands. "Horrible . . . it's a monster. . . ."

Boma, patting her shoulder, managed a wry grin. "We probably don't look so good to them, either."

Spock had gone to the forward window to look out of it. Something crashed against the hull. A great boulder tumbled past the window and rolled away to crash up against the side of the crater.

"All right, Spock," Boma said. "You have the answers. What now?"

Spock turned. "Your tone is hostile, Mr. Boma."

"My tone isn't the only thing that's hostile!"

"Strange," Spock mused. "Step by step I have done the logical thing."

McCoy blew up. "A little less analysis and a little more action! That's what we need!"

"How about analyzing what's happening to the plates of this craft?"

"The plates are titanite, Mr. Boma," Spock said. "They will hold. At least for a time."

"We have phasers. We could drive them off!"

"Mr. Boma, every ounce of energy in the phasers is needed by Mr. Scott. Were we to attack the creatures, the energy expended might well provide the very impetus required to secure our orbit."

The ship shook under another smash by a boulder—a bigger one, heavier, harder.

"How long, Mr. Scott?" Spock asked.

"Another hour. Maybe two."

"Can't you hurry it up?"

Scott raised an impatient face from his labor. "Doctor, a phaser will drain only so fast."

A steady, relentless hammering had begun on the hull. Boma, looking up, saw its plates vibrating. "How long can those plates hold out under *that?*" he cried. *"We've got to do something!"*

All eyes were on Spock. He met them directly, his own calm, as composed as though theirs contained no accusation.

Kirk lacked Spock's stoic capacity to tolerate helplessness. Though the ion storm was dispersing, the Starship's slow recovery of its operational power had tightened his nerves to the breaking point. He snapped at Uhura. "Lieutenant, what word from the sensor section?"

"At last report they were beginning to get readings, but they were completely scrambled."

"I'm not interested in the last report! I want the current one!"

"Yes, sir."

Kirk slammed his fist into his palm. When the elevator door opened, he didn't turn his head. He heard Ferris clear his throat. Then he was beside him, glancing ostentatiously at his watch. "You have three hours, Captain."

"I know the number of hours I have, Commissioner."

"Delighted to hear it. However, I shall continue to remind you."

"You do that," Kirk said.

Uhura spoke. "Sir, sensor section reporting. Static interference still creating false images. Estimate 80 percent undependable."

"Radio communication?"

"Clearing slowly but still incapable of transmission and reception."

"What do you intend to do?" demanded Ferris.

Kirk's overstrained control broke. "Do? I'll keep on searching, foot by foot, inch by inch . . . by candlelight if I have to, so long as I have a second left! And if you'll keep your nose off my bridge, I'll be thankful!"

"I'm sure your diligence will please the authorities, Captain. I am not sure they will appreciate the way you address a High Commissioner."

"I am in command here!"

"You are, Captain. For exactly—" he consulted his watch—"two hours and forty-two minutes."

Spock slammed no fist into his palm. The hammering by great rocks continued to shake the *Galileo*—but his Vulcan heritage forbade any release of tension building up in him. Boma's panic had now taken the form of an open scorn. Nor was there the slightest sign of sympathy in the others. Never had the half-human in Spock felt so lonely. But he gave no evidence of it as he said, "Mr. Scott, how much power do we have in our central batteries?"

"They're in good shape, sir. But they won't lift us off, if that's what you're getting at."

"Are they strong enough to electrify the exterior of the ship?"

A slow grin spread over Scott's face. "That they are, laddie." Reaching for some cables, he detached them.

Spock spoke to the others. "Get into the center of the ship. Don't touch the plates. Be sure you're insulated."

They obeyed, watching as Scott clamped an electrode to a metal projection on one side of the ship's interior. He was preparing the second electrode when a ferocious smash-down resounded from over their heads. Scott nodded at Spock.

"Stand by," Spock said.

The second electrode, attached, completed the circuit. Sparks flew up in a shower, followed by a wild shrieking of pain, shock and fury from outside the craft. The hammering stopped. Scott, releasing the electrodes, said, "I don't dare use any more power if we want to be sure of ignition."

Staring up at the silent hull, McCoy said, "It worked."

"For the moment," Spock said.

"For the moment?"

"Mr. Boma, they will return when they discover they're not seriously hurt. In the meantime, please check the aft compartment. See if there's anything else we can unload to lighten the ship."

Boma came back, grim-faced. "Gaetano's body is there."

"It will have to be left behind," Spock said.

"Not without a burial!"

"I would not recommend one, Mr. Boma. The creatures won't be far away." He paused. "A burial would expose the members of this crew to unnecessary peril."

"I'll take that chance," Boma said.

Spock looked at the alien human. "Do your vestigial ceremonies mean that much to you?"

"Spock, I would insist on a decent burial even if it were your body lying back there!"

"Mr. Boma!" It was McCoy's rebuke.

Boma whirled on him. "I'm sick and tired of this Vulcan machine!"

Scott had reddened with anger. "That's enough from you! Mr. Spock is a ranking Commander of the service!"

The ranking Commander spoke quietly. "You shall have your burial, Mr. Boma . . . if our friends permit it." McCoy, still smarting in Spock's behalf, moved over to him.

Landing party Two had beamed back to the *Enterprise* from Taurus II with casualties—one crewman dead, two wounded.

"Lieutenant Kelowitz, what happened?"

Kirk had activated the computer screen at Spock's station. Now it held the smudged, scratched image of the landing party's leader. Kirk could see that his uniform was torn.

"We were attacked, sir. Huge, furry creatures. I checked with astral anthropology. Order 480G, anthropoid, similar to life forms discovered on Hansen's planet—but much larger. Ten, twelve feet in height . . ."

"Your casualties?"

"Ensign O'Neill was speared even before we knew they were around. Crewman Immamura has a dislocated shoulder and severe lacerations, but he'll make it all right." The tired eyes on the screen were lost momentarily to horrified recollection of the monster anthropoids. "Captain, they're all over the place. If the *Galileo* is down on that planet . . ."

Kirk nodded. "Thank you, Lieutenant. You'd better report to Sickbay yourself."

"Aye, aye, sir."

The image faded—and Ferris strode out of the elevator, his jaw set. "Captain Kirk, if you will check your chronometer, you will see it is exactly 2823.8. Your time is up."

"Commissioner, my men are still out there," Kirk said.

"So are the plague victims on New Paris! I now assume the authority granted me under Title Fifteen, Galactic Emergency Procedures. I order you to abandon search, Captain."

Kirk said, "Shuttlecraft *Columbus* hasn't returned yet. I also have two search parties still out."

"You have your orders, Captain. Recall your search parties and proceed to Makus 111 immediately."

He was beaten.

His voice was inflectionless as he spoke to Uhura. "Lieutenant, order the Transporter Room to beam up the search parties still on the surface. Attempt contact with the *Columbus*."

"I'm in partial contact with them now, sir."

"Have them return at once." He left the computer station to return to his command chair. "Mr. Sulu, prepare to abandon search. Set course for Makus III."

Ferris left the bridge—and Kirk slumped back in his chair. There was nothing more to do, nothing more to say. Spock, McCoy, Scott—all dead, mercifully dead on that savage planet. Had their deaths been easy? Hardly. Uhura had to tell him twice that the sensor beams were working again.

No time to mourn. No time, period.

"The other systems?" he said to Uhura.

"No, sir. Still too much interference."

Sulu said, "Course set for Makus III, Captain."

"Thank you, Mr. Sulu. Steady on post. Lieutenant Uhura, how long before the *Columbus* comes aboard?"

"Twenty-three minutes, sir."

"Twenty-three minutes," Kirk said. Then, leaning his arms on his console, he cupped his chin in his hands.

Yeoman Mears, no longer fresh-faced, but tired and worn, had failed again to contact the *Enterprise*. She snapped closed her communicator. "Nothing, sir," she told Spock. "Just ionic interference."

He went to Scott. "How about weight?"

Scott finished draining the last phaser. He looked up as he laid it aside. "If we shed every extra ounce of it, we may be able to achieve orbit."

"How long can we keep it?"

"A few hours. If we time it right, we could cut out of orbit with enough fuel for a controlled re-entry."

"To land here again? Not an attractive possibility."

"We have very few alternatives," Scott said. He stooped to remove the drained phasers from the aisle as Boma and McCoy came from the aft compartment, carrying Gaetano's body.

"How does it look outside?" McCoy asked.

Spock glanced out the forward window. Then he spoke to Scott. "When can we lift off, Mr. Scott?"

"Maybe eight minutes if the weight's right."

Spock faced around from the window. "Doctor, Mr. Boma, the ship will lift off in exactly ten minutes. You have that long to bury Mr. Gaetano. It appears to be all clear outside, at least for the moment." He cautiously opened the hatch, peering around the crater. As he turned back inside, he said, "I shall assist you. Please hurry."

Yeoman Mears moved down the aisle to where Scott, at the control console, was warming up its equipment. "Can we get off?" she said.

"Oh, we can get off all right, lassie. But can we stay off? That's the question."

"If we make orbit, the *Enterprise* will—"

"By now," he said, "the *Enterprise* should be well on its way to Makus III."

"Then . . . we're alone."

"Not alone." He made a gesture toward the crater walls. "We've got some big hairy things out there to keep us company."

It was the thought of the big, hairy things that had brought Kirk to his decision. He uncupped his chin from his hands. "Mr. Sulu, proceed on course as ordered for Makus III. At space normal speed."

Sulu was startled. "But all systems report secured for warp factors, sir. Space normal speed?"

"You heard me, Mr. Sulu. Lieutenant Uhura, order all sensor sections to direct beams aft, full function, continuous operation until further orders."

Ferris, the paper man, had not specified warp speed.

They'd dug the grave in the spongy soil. It was as they were filling the hole that they all heard the grating sound. Then from the mist-shrouded rocks above them came a piercing howl—a triumphant roar as though the thing which had uttered it was beating its furry chest in token of victory.

"Into the ship!" Spock shouted. "Take-off immediate!"

A spear struck the grave. Another one grazed Boma's shoulder. Then the air was thick with them. Spock, racing toward the ship, saw a large axe of strange shape hit the ground. As he reached for it, a rock, hurtling down, crashed against his thigh. He struggled to rise but the wounded leg went out from under him. Dragging himself toward the ship, he yelled, "Lift off! Lift off!"

Boma and McCoy were at the open hatch. They left it to run to him. He waved them back furiously. "No! Get back! *Lift off!*"

They disobeyed. McCoy grabbed his shoulders—and a spear whizzed past his head. Half-carrying, half-pulling, they got Spock to the hatch and shoved him inside. Boma slammed it shut just as a giant body heaved at the craft, rocking it.

Spock, clutching his injured leg, glared at his rescuers. "I told you to lift off!"

McCoy, at work on the leg, said, "Don't be a fool, Spock. We couldn't leave you out there!" He paused. Once more, big rocks were hammering at the hull. Spock pushed McCoy away. "Can we lift off, Mr. Scott?"

"We should be able to—but we're not moving!"

Yeoman Mears screamed. In the port window beside her a bestial face, enormous, red-eyed was peering in at her. McCoy slammed the shutter down over the window. Spock was hobbling toward the console's seat. For a moment his delicate fingers flitted over the controls.

"They seem to be holding us down," he said. "All systems are go—but we're not moving." His hand went out to another switch. Appalled, Scott cried, "What are you doing, man?"

"The boosters."

"We won't be able to hold orbit!"

Spock moved the switch. The ship bucked. Needles quivered on the console. There was a last defiant crash on the hull, screams of baffled hate—and the *Galileo* shot up and out of the crater.

Yeoman Mears burst into tears of relief. "We're rid of them . . . of that terrible place. . . ."

Spock spoke. "I must remind you all that we have yet to achieve orbit. Nor can we maintain it long. An hour from now we might well be right back where we started."

But Spock's warning couldn't depress the hope roused by the familiar sight of star-filled space. McCoy, thoughtfully regarding the straight back in the console's seat, said, "Spock—back there—what held you back when we were attacked?"

"A most intriguing artifact . . . a hand axe, Doctor, reminiscent of those used by the Lake People of Athos IV."

"Even if you'd gotten it, you couldn't have brought it back with you. It must have weighed a hundred and fifty pounds."

Spock looked around from the console, his face astounded. "You know, Doctor, until this moment, that never occurred to me."

McCoy grunted. "An encouraging sign of humanity. It was a fool thing to do. It almost got you killed. If we hadn't come after you . . ."

"By coming after me you caused a delay in our lift off. So you may well have destroyed what slim chance you have of survival. The logical thing was to leave me behind."

McCoy sighed. "Well, you're back to normal. Remind me to tell you sometime how sick and tired I am of your logic."

"I will, Doctor." He was scanning the console. "Orbit attitude in one minute, Mr. Scott. Fuel status?"

"Fifteen pounds psi. Approximately enough for one complete orbit."

"And after that?" McCoy said.

Scott shook his head. "Tapping those boosters removed our last chance of making a soft landing."

"You mean—a burn-up?" asked Boma.

Spock said, "That is the usual end of a decaying orbit."

McCoy got up and went to him. "Spock, can't we do anything?"

He looked up. "The *Enterprise* is undoubtedly back on course for Makus III. I, for one, do not believe in angels. There won't be one around, Doctor, to bear us up on its wings."

"Well, Spock . . . so ends your first command."

"Yes. My first command."

Scott said, "Orbit attitude attained, Mr. Spock. With present fuel that gives us about forty-five minutes."

But Spock seemed singularly uninterested in the information. Nodding slightly, he stared at the console. Then he slowly turned his head to look at the others. They were all back there in their seats . . . McCoy, the girl, Boma—and Scott, standing by. And all of them, each in his own way, alone with the thought of the final extinction. But their eyes were on him as though he could magically avert it for them. If he'd been a sweating creature, Spock would have been wet with it. Instead, he was a Vulcan by training as well as inheritance, a being required to remain impervious to emotion. Now, in his half-human agony, he took refuge behind a mask of stone. His first and last command. His hand went out toward a switch.

"Spock!" Scott shouted.

He threw the switch. The ship trembled—and a blast of fire burst from its pods.

"What's happened?" cried the girl.

"He's jettisoned the fuel—and ignited it!" Scott yelled.

Boma was on his feet. "Have you gone crazy, Spock?"

"Perhaps, Mr. Boma."

McCoy, licking his lips, girded himself for the question. "Scotty, how long do we have?"

"Six minutes."

At Sulu's cry Kirk turned his pain-drawn face. "Yes, Mr. Sulu?"

"The screen, Captain! Something's back there! At Taurus II!"

The strain had been too much for all of them. Sulu was hallucinating. "The screen," Kirk said. Then he looked at it. "Sensors, Mr. Sulu? A meteorite?"

"No, sir. It's holding a lateral line! There it is again ... on the screen. Captain, it's holding steady!"

A streak of flame was moving against the blackness of space.

Kirk exploded into action. "One hundred and eighty degrees about, Mr. Sulu! Lieutenant Uhura! Contact Transporter Room! All beams ready! Full normal speed!"

On the screen the flame flickered—and died.

And on the *Galileo* Spock sat unmoving. The heat had begun. He could sense the unbelieving eyes fixed on him—on his Satanic, alien ears. He had destroyed them. He was hardly aware of the hand, the human hand, that suddenly fell on his shoulder.

"Ah, laddie," Scott said, "it was a good gamble. Maybe it was worth it."

Somebody said, "I don't ... understand."

Scott whirled. "He turned the ship into a distress signal—a flare!"

Spock said, "Even if there's no one out there to see it."

Scott kept the hand on his shoulder. "The orbit's decaying. Thirty-six seconds to atmosphere."

McCoy joined them. "It may be the last action you ever take, Spock—but it was all human."

"Totally illogical, Doctor. There was no chance."

"Which is exactly what I mean," McCoy said.

A whining sound came. A wisp of smoke drifted from the control panel. Spock, reaching up, slid up the metal shutter on the forward window. The *Galileo* was on fire, glowing red to orange to pure white flame. Its prisoners tore at their throats, coughing as the aisle filled with hot smoke.

Kirk, fingers crossed in the old Earth's plea to Lady Luck, said, *"Activate Transporter beams!"*

Then he waited. A sweating creature, he could feel it breaking from every pore of his body. Sulu said, "Whatever it was, Captain, it just burned up in the atmosphere."

"Yes. I can see for myself, Mr. Sulu."

Behind him Uhura leaped from her chair. "Captain! Transporter Room reports five persons aboard! Alive and well!"

"Alive, Lieutenant?"

So the beams had caught them. In the searing heat of the *Galileo*, they had faded, breaking to the dazzle that had brought them home. Kirk covered his face with his hands. Then he lifted his head. "Mr. Sulu. Proceed on course for Makus 111. Warp factor one."

"Aye, aye, sir. Warp factor one."

McCoy was whispering to Kirk. Then they both looked over to the computer station where Spock sat, composed, his eyes intent on his dials.

"Mr. Spock?"

"Yes, Captain."

"When you ignited all your remaining fuel, you knew there was virtually no chance the flame would be seen. But you did it anyhow. Am I correct in defining that as an act of desperation?"

"Yes, Captain."

"Desperation is a highly emotional state of mind. How do you account for it in yourself?"

"Quite simply, sir. I examined the problem from all angles. It was plainly hopeless. Logic informed me that the only possible action would have to be a desperate one. A logical decision, logically arrived at."

"You mean, you reasoned it was time for an emotional outburst?"

"I would not use those terms, sir, but those are essentially the facts."

"You're not going to admit that for once in your life you committed a purely human, emotional act?"

"No, sir."

"Mr. Spock, you are a stubborn man."

"Yes, sir."

Kirk got up, started toward him, thought better of it. Grinning, he shook his head, himself accepting the logic of facts as they were. Spock caught the grin. His left eyebrow lifted.

IS THERE IN TRUTH NO BEAUTY?

(Jean Lisette Aroeste)

The civilian named Lawrence Marvick stepped from the Transporter platform of the *Enterprise,* aggression in every line of his square-jawed face. Kirk, moving forward to greet him, thought, *What's the man afraid of?* But his voice was smoothly cordial. "Welcome aboard, Mr. Marvick. I am James Kirk, the Cap—"

Marvick cut him off. "Kirk, what are you doing here? You'll have to leave, you know, before the Medeusan Ambassador arrives!"

"I am aware of that, Mr. Marvick. We have taken all precautions. This is Mr. Spock, our First Officer."

Marvick eyed Spock briefly. "Oh yes, you're the Vulcan. It's all right for you to remain here but you, Kirk, and that other officer . . ."

Scott came from the Transporter console to shake the guest's hand with enthusiasm. "Montgomery Scott, Chief Engineer, Mr. Marvick. Call me Scotty!"

Recovering his hand, the new arrival addressed Spock. "Have you got your vizor? You must have it. Humans who get even a glimpse of Medeusans have gone insane."

Spock bowed. "Thank you, Mr. Marvick. I shall be wearing the vizor."

Marvick's authoritative manner was beginning to rile Kirk. "We mustn't keep the Ambassador waiting," he said. "Mr. Marvick, will you go with Mr. Scott now, please? You two should have a good deal in common."

As Scott ushered the man out, Kirk heard him say, "It's a rare privilege to meet one of the designers of the *Enterprise.* I appreci—"

The door closed and Kirk crossed to the intercom. "Lieutenant Uhura, inform the Ambassador and Dr. Jones that we're ready to beam them aboard." He turned

IS THERE IN TRUTH NO BEAUTY? 83

to see Spock removing a red safety vizor from his belt. "You're sure that thing will work?"

"It has proved entirely effective for Vulcans, sir."

"It's your human half I'm worried about. Report to me when the Transport has been completed."

"Yes, Captain."

Left alone as the Captain returned to the bridge, Spock adjusted the vizor. It covered not only his eyes but the whole upper half of his face. At the Transporter console, he manipulated the beam-up buttons. On the platform sparkles gradually assumed the slim shape of a young woman. The sheen of embroidery on her long, graceful gown matched her cloud of silver-blond hair. Beside her was a box of medium size. Removing her red vizor, she revealed black-lashed eyes of a vivid blue. Then, to Spock's astonishment, a white arm was lifted in the Vulcan salute.

An eyebrow slightly raised, Spock returned it. "Welcome aboard, Ambassador Kollos," he said. "I am First Officer Spock."

She stepped from the platform. "And I am Dr. Jones —Dr. Miranda Jones." She gestured to the box still on the platform. "The Ambassador is honored to meet you."

Quiet and undisconcerted, Spock went to the box, affixing anti-gravs to it. When they were firmly clamped into place, he made his report to Kirk. "Ready to proceed, Captain."

Kirk, on the bridge, swung to Uhura. "Lieutenant, open channels to all decks."

"All channels open, sir."

Kirk reached for his speaker. "This is the Captain. All ship's personnel, clearance plans now in effect. Vacate corridors immediately. The Ambassador will be escorted at once to his quarters." He moved an intercom button. "Mr. Spock, all decks are now clear. You may proceed."

The box was clearly the habitat of the Medeusan Ambassador. As Spock lifted it carefully out of an elevator, he said, "Dr. Jones, may I offer you my congratulations on your assignment with Ambassador Kollos?"

She bowed. "The assignment is not yet definite. It will depend upon my ability to achieve a true mind-link with the Ambassador."

"You should find it a fascinating experience."

A flicker of resentment flashed in her blue eyes. "I wasn't aware that *anyone* had ever succeeded in a mind-link with a Medeusan!"

"Nobody has," Spock said. "I was merely referring to mind-links I have attempted with other species."

"Surely," she said, "your duties as a Starship officer do not permit you the luxury of many such experiments!"

He regarded her gravely. "My duties as a Starship officer permit me very few luxuries of any kind."

She reached for a conciliatory tone. "You make it quite obvious that the *Enterprise* is your paramount interest." She paused before she added, "You know, Mr. Spock, I have heard you turned down this assignment with Ambassador Kollos."

"I could not accept it," he said. "As you've pointed out, my life is here. And the Ambassador's quarters are also here." He indicated a cabin on their right.

There was a pedestal in the cabin. Setting the habitat down on it, Spock removed the anti-gravs. At the room's intercom, he said, "Spock to bridge. We have reached the Ambassador's quarters, Captain."

"Thank you, Mr. Spock. Lieutenant Uhura, notify all hands to return to stations." Kirk sighed with relief as he turned to Sulu. "All right, helmsman. Let's take her out. Warp factor two."

"Warp factor two, sir."

In the cabin, Spock, vizored like Miranda, was eyeing the alien habitat. "Dr. Jones," he said, "I should very much like to exchange greetings with Ambassador Kollos."

She smiled. "I am sure the Ambassador will be charmed."

Both of them placed a hand on the box. Then they went perfectly still, each absorbed in deep concentration. After a long moment the lid of the box lifted very slightly —and a light of purest blue streamed through the crack. Leaning forward, Spock peered into the box. Instantly, he recoiled; but after pausing to recover from the sight, he looked into it again. His lips moved in a smile of an almost childlike wonder.

The girl saw the smile. Once more resentment flashed

in her eyes. The lid of the box fell. Unsmiling now, Spock said, "I almost envy you your assignment, Dr. Jones."

"Do I read in your thoughts that you are tempted to take my place, Mr. Spock?"

"No. But I feel your mind trying to touch mine, Doctor. Were you born a telepath?"

She nodded. "Yes. That is why I had to study on Vulcan."

"Of course," he said. "May I now show you to your quarters?"

"I'd better remain here a bit. Ambassador Kollos sometimes finds the process of Transport unsettling."

"Our ship's surgeon often makes the same complaint." He pointed to the intercom. "Call when you are ready."

He bowed and left the cabin. Miranda turned back to the habitat. She removed her vizor roughly, her beautiful face disturbed, doubtful, even apprehensive. In the solitude of the cabin, she cried out fiercely, "What did he see when he looked at you, Kollos? I have to know! I have to know!"

The *Enterprise* had done itself proud. Though dinner was over, hosts and guests still lingered over their brandy at a table elegant with crystal, candlelight, arrangements of fresh-cut flowers. All the officers wore dress uniforms; and Miranda, in silver-embroidered blue velvet, glowed like a blond pearl in the candlelight. Marvick, in civilian white tie and tails, was quiet but observant.

Kirk refilled the girl's brandy goblet. "I can't understand," he said, "why they're letting you go with Kollos."

"*They*, Captain?"

"The male population of the Federation. Didn't anyone try to talk you out of it?"

The black lashes drooped. "Well . . . now that you ask, yes."

"I'm glad he didn't succeed," Kirk said. "If he had, I'd never have met you." He raised his glass to her. "Tell me, Dr. Jones, why isn't it dangerous for you to be with Kollos? Spock I can understand. Nothing makes any impression on him."

"Why, thank you, Captain," Spock said.

"Not at all, Mr. Spock." He turned back to Miranda. "No other human is able to look at Kollos without going mad, even when vizored. How do you manage?"

"I spent four years on Vulcan studying their mental disciplines."

McCoy spoke. "You poor girl!" he cried with heartfelt sympathy.

Spock looked down the table at him. "Indeed, Doctor! I would say that the lady is very fortunate!"

"Vulcan disciplines are hardly *my* idea of fun."

"On Vulcan," the girl said, "I learned to do what it is impossible to learn anywhere else."

Smiling, Kirk asked, "How to read minds?"

"How *not* to read them, Captain."

"I'm afraid I don't understand," Kirk said.

Spock interposed. "Dr. Jones was born a telepath, Captain."

Miranda laughed. "Vulcan was necessary to my sanity, Captain! I had to learn how to close out the thoughts of others."

Spock nodded. "What humans generally find it impossible to understand is the need to shut out the bedlam of others' thoughts and emotions."

"Not to mention the bedlam of even one's *own* emotions," Miranda said. "On Vulcan one learns to do that, too." She reached out to touch a medallion pinned to Spock's breast. McCoy watched her fingers move over it.

Spock pulled back, fearful of scratching her. "Forgive me," he said. "I forget that dress uniforms can injure."

She leaned toward him. "I was merely interested in your Vulcan IDIC, Mr. Spock. Is it a reminder that you could mind-meld with the Ambassador much more effectively than I could?"

There was an uncomfortable pause. She broke it hastily, explaining, "It would be most difficult for a Vulcan to see a mere human take on this exciting challenge, gentlemen."

"Interesting," McCoy said. "It's a fact, Spock, that you rarely wear your IDIC."

"Bones," Kirk said, "I doubt that our First Officer

would don the most revered of all Vulcan symbols merely to annoy a guest."

Spock spoke for himself, looking straight at Miranda. "In fact, I wear it this evening to honor you, Dr. Jones."

"Indeed?" she said.

"Yes," he said, "indeed. Perhaps, despite those years on Vulcan, you missed the true symbology of the IDIC." He placed his hand on the medallion. "The triangle and the circle . . . different shapes, materials, textures . . . they represent any two diverse things which come together to create truth or beauty." He rose, brandy glass in hand. "For example—Dr. Miranda Jones, who has combined herself with the disciplines of my race to become greater than the sum of both!"

Suddenly uneasy, Kirk saw that his lovely guest appreciated neither the grace nor the sincerity of Spock's gallantry. He changed the subject. "Back to your mission, Dr. Jones. Do you feel a way can be found to employ Medeusan navigators on Starships? It would solve many of our present navigational problems."

"The key is the mind-link learned on Vulcan. Once we learn to form a corporate intelligence with Medeusans, designers of Starships—and that's where Larry Marvick comes in—can work on adapting instruments."

McCoy stirred in his chair. "I don't care how 'benevolent' the Medeusans are supposed to be. Isn't it suicidal to deal with something ugly enough to cause madness? Why do you do it?"

"Dr. McCoy," Spock said, "I see that you still subscribe to the outmoded notion held by your ancient Greeks—the one which insists that what is good must also be beautiful."

Marvick spoke for the first time. "And the obverse of it—that what is beautiful is automatically expected to be good."

"I suppose," Kirk reflected, "that most of us are naturally attracted by beauty as we are repelled by ugliness. It's the last of our predjudices. But at the risk of sounding prejudiced—" He paused to raise his glass to Miranda. "Here's to Beauty!"

All the men rose and drank. McCoy lifted his glass

a second time. "To Miranda Jones—the loveliest woman ever to grace a Starship!" He looked around at his fellow males. "How can one so beautiful condemn herself to look upon ugliness for the rest of her life? Will we allow it?"

His answer was a general shout of "No!"

McCoy sat down. "We must not permit her to leave us!"

Miranda was smiling at him. "How can one so full of the love of life as you, Dr. McCoy, condemn himself to look upon suffering and disease for the rest of his life? Can we allow *that*, gentlemen?"

McCoy tipped his glass to her, sipping from it. "I drink to whatever it is you want most, Miranda."

As Kirk joined in the toast, he noticed how intently Marvick was staring at the girl. He was about to offer her more brandy when he was halted by the look of terror that had abruptly come into her face.

She rose to her feet, crying, "There's a murd—" She broke off and the flower she had been holding dropped to the table.

Kirk caught her arm. "Dr. Jones, what is it?" But McCoy was already beside her. "You're ill," he said. "Let me help you. . . ."

She pulled away, her face slightly calmer. "There's someone nearby thinking of murder," she said.

Shocked silence fell over the table. She was clearly serious and Kirk said, "Who is it—can you tell?"

"It's . . . not there now. I . . . I can't pick it up at all."

"Was it in this room?" Kirk said.

She looked around her. "I don't know, Captain. It's gone now." She seemed to have regained her composure. "These things are usually momentary. A common human impulse, seldom acted out."

Spock's quiet voice said, "True. Otherwise the human race would have ceased to exist."

"Captain, do you mind if I say good night now? I'd love to visit your herbarium—but another time, if I may."

"Of course, Dr. Jones. I'll see you back to—"

Spock interrupted. "Perhaps I could see you back to your quarters?"

McCoy was staring curiously at her. "Thank you, gentlemen," she said. "You make a choice impossible. Please stay here and enjoy yourselves. It was a delightful dinner."

"Sleep well, Miranda," Kirk said.

She waved a friendly good night to them. But McCoy, who was still watching her closely, went quickly to her at the door. "Are you sure you're well enough to find your way alone?"

"Yes, Dr. McCoy. Please don't worry about me."

McCoy bowed and, reaching for her hand, kissed it lightly. As the door closed behind her, he said, "Where I come from, that's what's called a 'lady.' "

"She *is* something special," Kirk agreed.

"*Very special!* I suggest you treat her accordingly!"

Marvick's sudden outburst startled them all. The man picked up a napkin and dropped it. "I—I have not known Dr. Jones for a long time. But long enough to be aware of her remarkable gifts!" He paused. "Well, it's been a long day for me . . ."

Scott said, "Would you like to stop off in Engineering, Larry? I have a few things to check; and a bottle of Scotch says you can't handle the controls you designed."

"Some other time," Marvick told him.

The door closed behind him. Turning away from it, Kirk looked Spock over. "Spock, you're really dressed up for the occasion. Very impressive."

"I genuinely intended to honor her, Captain." He moved to the door. "Good night, gentlemen."

His face unusually thoughtful, McCoy was still standing at the closed door. He looked at Kirk's handsome face. "That's not just another girl, Jim. Don't make that mistake."

Kirk grinned. "I can see that for myself, Bones. Anything else?"

"I can't say exactly what it is. She seems very . . . vulnerable."

Kirk was smiling again. "We're all vulnerable, Dr. McCoy . . . in one way or another."

"Yes. But there is something very disturbing about her."

"You'll get no argument from me, Bones. Meaning that she's quite a woman."

"Good night, Jim," McCoy said.

Alone, Kirk returned to the table. He retrieved the flower she had dropped and tucked it into the breast of his uniform.

Miranda's cabin was luxurious. She drifted around it, graceful but aimless, occasionally touching objects, perhaps because she admired them, perhaps to acquaint herself with the room's dimensions and contents. A buzz at her door sounded.

She leaned against it, calling, "Who is it?"

"Larry. I've got to talk to you."

"Larry, it's late. . . ."

"Please, Miranda. It's important."

She opened the door. "All right. Come in, then."

Marvick's face had the haunted look of a man in desperate need of a drug. Closing the door behind him, he stood silent for a moment, looking at the girl. "I thought that dinner," he said, "was never going to end."

He moved closer to her. She backed away, putting distance between them. "I rather enjoyed it," she said.

"I know you did. I didn't. You were too far away."

"Larry, I'll be further away than that soon." Her tone was intended to be soothing. But it failed to soothe. "Don't speak of that!" Marvick cried. "Don't . . . no, we have to speak of it. There is so little time. . . ." He reached for her but she eluded him, maintaining the little distance. "Please, Miranda, don't go with Kollos!"

She sighed. "Larry, we've been over that time and time again. Please accept—"

Marvick tried for lightness but his hunger broke through it. "Don't I know? I've begged you in restaurants, in the laboratory, on one knee, on both knees! Miranda, how can you do this to me?"

"If you would only try to understand . . ."

"What I understand is that you're a woman and I'm a man—one of your own kind! You think that Kollos will ever be able to give you anything like this?" He had her in his arms. The kiss crushed her lips against her teeth. Then his violence suddenly ended. He held her quietly, caressing her hair, her throat, blind to the quickened anger in her eyes.

She freed herself. "You shouldn't have done that," she said coldly.

He ran a distracted hand over his face. "I'm sorry. . . . "Why, oh why did I ever meet you?"

"I have been honest with you," she said. "I simply cannot love you the way you want me to. And I am going with Kollos. That is final."

"Miranda, in God's name . . . !"

She went to the door. "I think you'd better leave now. I find you exhaust—" She suddenly broke off. Her hand went to her mouth to block a scream.

"So it's you!" she cried.

He lowered his head like an animal at bay. She was at the far side of the room now, her face white with shock. "I didn't know it was you before! Who is it you want to kill, Larry? Me? Larry, you must not keep such impulses to yourself! I can help you. . . ."

"So now you want to 'help' me, do you? Well, now I know what a man has to do to get a response from you! A patient is what you want—not a man! Dr. Jones, the great psychologist! Just for a change of pace, try to be a woman for once in your life!"

He slammed the door behind him. Outside at the elevator, he turned and went back. At her cabin, he hesitated before moving on down the corridor. His square jaw hard, he stopped at the door of the Medeusan's quarters. Firmly and deliberately, he pushed it open.

In the cabin's center the habitat still stood on its pedestal. It emitted a steady, pulsing sound. For a moment Marvick stood, tense, his back to it, hand on the door handle. Then he turned to look at the box, his eyes blazing with hatred. The pulsing sound grew louder, as though the box's occupant had been aroused to danger.

There was an instant when fear and fascination combined to immobilize Marvick. It passed. His hand went fast to the phaser at his belt. The lid of the habitat flashed open, enveloping Marvick in blinding light. He staggered, dropping the phaser. The Medeusan reared up. Marvick screamed as his hand whipped up to shield his eyes from the forbidden sight of Kollos.

Miranda sat bolt upright on her sleeping couch. Then her hand went to her throat. Leaping from the couch, she flew to her cabin door. Panic ran with her as she raced down the corridor to Kollos's quarters.

In his light that still filled the room, she saw the phaser. Tears flooded her eyes. Arms outstretched, she went close to the habitat, crying, "Forgive me! Kollos, forgive me!"

The rhythm of the pulsing slowed.

Down in Engineering, Scott was adjusting a control, a yeoman at work nearby. The yeoman turned as the door opened, saw Marvick and signaled Scott. Scott beamed. "Ah, there you are, Larry! So you couldn't resist that little wager!"

Trembling, still in shock, Miranda had found the cabin's intercom. Kirk, listening to her incoherent whispers, jumped from his command chair, shouting, "Lieutenant Uhura, Mr. Spock and Dr. McCoy on the double! The Ambassador's quarters! Notify Security!"

He found two guards already at the door. He banged on it, calling, "Miranda ... Miranda!"

Spock was arranging his vizor as the door opened. The girl, her own vizor in place, seemed to have recovered some composure. Silently, she passed the phaser to Kirk, lifting the mask from her eyes.

"Has the Ambassador been hurt?"

"No harm was done to him, Captain."

"Do you know who would do such a thing?"

"Larry Marvick."

Kirk stared. "Marvick? But why?"

"Madness prompted him."

Spock spoke quickly. "Did he see the Medeusan?"

"Yes, Mr. Spock."

"Then insanity is the certain result. Dangerous insanity, Captain."

Kirk ran for the cabin intercom. While he ordered a Red Alert, Scott was turning the ship's controls over to Marvick. "They're all yours, Larry. That Scotch will be in your cabin tonight if you can handle them!"

Kirk's filtered voice reached Engineering. "Captain Kirk to all ship personnel. An attempt has been made to murder Ambassador Kollos. The man is dangerously insane. He is Lawrence Marvick. Be on the watch for him. Kirk out."

Scott's jaw fell. Pulling himself together, he tried to push Marvick away from the controls, but the man's joined fists came crashing down on him with all the force of madness. Scott crumpled. The yeoman leaped for Marvick's back and was smashed to the deck.

The ship groaned under the lash of sudden acceleration. Staggering, Kirk, Spock and McCoy looked at each other. The ship's groan had become a whine when they raced out of the bridge elevator.

"Explain, Mr. Sulu!" Kirk shouted.

"I can't, sir. But we're traveling at warp factor eight point five."

"And still accelerating, Captain," Chekov said.

Spock looked at the helm console. "Our deflectors can't hold unless speed is immediately reduced."

"Lieutenant Uhura, put me through to Engineering!"

She turned to her console, bracing herself against the ship's shuddering. "Captain, they don't answer...."

Sulu said, "Warp factor nine, accelerating."

Kirk wheeled to Spock. "Mr. Spock, can you disengage the power from here?"

Spock already lay on his back, reaching inside a wall panel. "We shall try to, Captain. Mr. Chekov, come here, please. I need you."

Uhura turned. "I seem to have Engineering, Captain."

"Put it on the intercom, Lieutenant."

He heard Marvick's voice. It was singing. "We'll make it! We're under way now! We'll make it—and get out of here!"

A maniacal laugh echoed through the bridge.

Kirk hit the intercom. "Security! Get down to Engineering!"

Miranda appeared at his elbow. "I'll go with you," she said.

"No."

"I must, Captain. I can reach his mind."

After a moment, he nodded.

In the corridor outside Engineering, two Security guards were trying to open the door. "He's jammed it, Captain," one said. "But with another good pull..."

It opened. Marvick, at the controls, was manipulating them easily and skillfully. But his dementia was unmistakable. Moans of genuine anguish were followed by seizures of uncontrollable giggles. When he saw Kirk standing quietly beside him, he chuckled. "Don't worry, Kirk. We'll be safe soon. Over the boundaries of the universe. We can hide there...."

Kirk made a grab for the controls and Sulu's voice said, "Warp speed nine point five and accelerating, Captain."

Marvick had lashed out at Kirk with a thick metal tool. The guards closed in on him, pinning his furiously flailing arms behind his back. Scott, crawling to his feet, was moving groggily toward the controls when the ship broke out of the galaxy. In a flash of searing light, the shapes of people, instruments—everything—dissolved into nameless colors, confused and changing. A roar so deafening it lost the quality of sound hammered at the trembling *Enterprise*. The ship stopped, hanging suspended in a space of alien colors.

Kirk had been flung across the deck. As the roar diminished, he got slowly to his feet. Marvick, still held tight by the guards, was whispering, "We're safe. We made it. We're safe, Kirk. We made it over the boundaries of the galaxy."

McCoy was on his knees. Kirk nodded to him. Bones hauled himself up and, opening his medikit, stepped behind Marvick. But the hypo's needle had barely touched him when he made a lunge that almost broke the guards' hold.

Kirk said, "Marvick, it will help you sleep."

The tortured creature shrieked. "No! No! We mustn't sleep! Never! Never again. No sleep! Never! They come into your dreams. Then they can suffocate you! No sleep —no dreams. No! No!"

Kirk went to him. "All right, Larry. No sleep. No dreams. Just come with me. I have a better hiding place for you. I'll take you to it. Come...."

Marvick made another break for the controls. "We must be ready to speed, Kirk! Speed! Speed on to the next galaxy. Away from here! Away!"

The wildly roving eyes caught sight of Miranda. Marvick tore his arms free and stretched them out to her. Then he collapsed. Kirk nodded to the guards, who released him. Supporting the limp body in his own arms, Kirk saw that Marvick's eyes had filled with tears. "Miranda . . . Miranda," he was whispering. "You . . . are here . . . with me. . . ."

Kirk carried him to a bench. The girl came to kneel beside Marvick. "Yes, Larry," she said. "I am here."

The madman cupped her face in his hands. "I didn't lose you. My beautiful love. I thought I . . . had lost you."

"I am here, Larry."

For the first time, Kirk saw the depth of Marvick's love. The tears were wet on the man's face and his body was trembling. Miranda looked up at Kirk. "I see what he sees," she said and, turning back to Marvick, spoke softly. "Don't, Larry. Don't think of what you saw. Don't think of it. . . ."

He uttered a scream of pain, pushing her away. "Liar! Deceiver! You're not alone! He's here! He's here! You brought him with you!"

The jealous hate rose in him again. He caught the girl by the throat. The Security guards moved quickly to help Kirk loosen his clutch. This time McCoy was fast with his hypo.

Kirk lifted Miranda in his arms. Watching them, Marvick spoke quietly. "Do not love her. She will kill you if you love her. Do not love her."

Kirk looked down at the woman in his arms, the warning in his ears. He carried her to the door when the dying man behind him called, "I love you, Miranda. . . ."

"Where are we, Mr. Spock?"

The bridge viewing screen showed only tangles of those alien, nameless, ever-changing colors. Spock lifted his head from hard work at his library computer. "Far outside our own galaxy, Captain, judging from the lack of any traceable reference points."

"What you mean is we're nowhere," Chekov said.

Nowhere. Kirk moved restlessly in his command chair as McCoy, a paper in his hand, came out of the elevator.

"May I interrupt, Jim?"

"Yes, Bones."

"I've got the autopsy on Marvick. Heart stopped: cause unknown. Brain activity stopped: cause unknown. ... Shall I go on?"

"You mean he simply died?"

"I mean he evidently couldn't live with what he saw."

Kirk looked unseeingly at the screen. "Or with what he felt." Remembering the mad eyes dripping tears, Kirk sighed. Nowhere. But back to business just the same. He turned to Scott. "How much damage to the engines, Scotty?"

"We'll need some repairs, sir, but the ship is basically intact."

"Mr. Spock, can you at least give us a position report?"

"Impossible to calculate, Captain. We lack data to analyze. Our instruments seem to function normally but what they tell us makes no sense." He paused. "Our records are reasonably clear up to the point at which we left our galaxy."

"We should be able to navigate back."

"We have no reference points to use in plotting a return course, Captain. We experienced extreme sensory distortion; and will do so again if we try to use warp speed. Nor can we recross the barrier at sublight speed."

"A madman got us into this and it's beginning to look as if only a madman can get us out."

"An entertaining suggestion, Mr. Chekov," Spock said. "Unhelpful, however."

Kirk rose and went to Spock. "The Medeusans have developed interstellar navigation to a fine art. Could Kollos function as a navigator in spite of the sensory distortion?"

"Very possibly, sir. The Medeusan's sensory system is radically different from ours. Perhaps, for the purpose of this emergency, I could become Kollos. And he become Spock."

"Explain."

"A fusion, Captain. A mind-link to create a double entity. Each of us will possess the knowledge and capabilities of both. We will function as one being."

"What are the hazards?"

"If the link is successful, there'll be a tendency to lose separate identity. It is a necessary risk." He hesitated, his eyes on Kirk's. "Of course, the lady will not want to give me permission to establish the link."

"I don't think she'd want *anyone* to intrude on the kind of rapport she has with Kollos," McCoy said.

"Dr. Jones," Spock said, "has shown reluctance whenever I have asked to converse with Kollos. In some ways she is still most human, Captain. Particularly in the vigor of her jealousy and her thirst for power."

Kirk didn't speak, and Spock went on. "Her telepathic powers are also formidable. If it is at all possible, her mind must be so engaged that no other thoughts will intrude on it."

"I think that can be arranged," Kirk said.

McCoy looked at him. "Jim, don't take this lightly. She's extremely sensitive. If you try to be devious with her, she'll know."

"Bones, I know what's at stake. I have no intention of playing games with Miranda."

He turned on his heel and left the bridge.

The Starship's herbarium was odorous with the mingled scents of flowers.

Kirk released Miranda's arm. "I may be sentimental, but this is my favorite room. It reminds me of Earth."

"I've never been to Earth. But what lovely flowers! May I touch them, Captain?"

He smiled at her. "Go ahead."

She moved down the path, stopping to stroke a velvety petal, a leaf. Watching her, Kirk thought: *She's a blossom herself*. But a spray of butterfly orchids disappointed her. "They have no scent," she complained, turning to Kirk.

"Try these."

They were roses, white, yellow, pale pink, some nearly black. She plunged her face into them, inhaling their perfume with delight. Suddenly she cried out, pulled away and with a grimace of pain put her hurt finger to her mouth.

Kirk took her hand. "Let me see. . . ."

"It was just a thorn," she said hastily, removing the hand. Kirk recovered it. Gently, he rubbed her finger. "I was hoping to make you forget about thorns today," he said.

"It doesn't hurt anymore."

"You mustn't blame yourself," he said, "because Marvick loved you."

Her abrupt ferocity startled him. "I don't! I didn't want his love! I couldn't return it—and I had no use for it!"

Kirk spoke slowly. "Surely, sooner or later you will want human love—a man to companion you."

She pushed aside a strand of silver-blond hair. "Shall I tell you what human companionship means to me? A battle! Defense against others' emotions! When I'm tired and my guard slips, their feelings burst in on me like a storm. Hatred, desire, envy, pity—pity's the worst of all! I agree with the Vulcans. Violent emotion is a kind of insanity."

"So you will spend the rest of your life with Medeusans to avoid human feelings?"

"Perhaps."

"A meeting of minds isn't enough. What are you going to do for love hunger, Miranda?"

She turned her back on him. "You will never understand me. I don't think you should try, Captain."

He pulled her around to face him. "Look. You are young, human. No matter how beautiful the Medeusans' minds are, they are alien to yours! You'll yearn for the sight and sound of a human like yourself—and weary of ugliness!"

The black-lashed eyes blazed. "Ugly! What *is* ugly? You have never seen Kollos! Who are you to say whether he is too ugly to bear or too beautiful to bear?"

"I did not mean to insult you. Please, Miranda. . . ."

As she ripped a leaf from the rosebush beside her, Spock was striding down the corridor to Kollos's cabin.

Kirk wasn't a man to be fazed by female tantrums. He picked up the leaf she'd flung down. "Well," he said, "we can agree upon one thing, anyway. We both like roses. I wish I had moonlight for you, too. I'd like to see what moonlight would do to that hair of yours." He reached for her but she evaded him with a little laugh.

"I see you're a very complicated man, Captain."

He had her, unresisting, in his arms. "Play fair," he whispered into the ear on his shoulder. "You're not supposed to know what I'm thinking about. I'm supposed to show you."

He felt her stiffen. She released herself with a surprising strength. "He's with Kollos!" she cried. "Oh no, you mustn't let him do it!" She turned and ran down the path. He caught her. "Miranda! You can't leave just as . . ."

She tore herself free. "Let me go! You don't realize! You don't know what a dangerous thing Spock is planning! Please, please, we must stop him!"

Kirk followed her at a run.

Spock was standing at the door of the Medeusan's quarters. He turned as they burst out of the elevator. Miranda tried to shove him aside. Grave, entirely composed, he looked at her. "The *Enterprise* is at stake, Dr. Jones. It is not possible for you to be involved."

"Why? I've already committed myself to mind-link with Kollos!" She whirled to Kirk. "Why do you allow him to place himself in jeopardy?"

"Mine is a duty you cannot assume," Spock said. "The vital factor to be considered is not telepathic competence. It is to pilot this ship. That is something you cannot do."

"Then teach me to pilot it! I can memorize instantly. Set any test you choose. After only one rehearsal, I shall be able to operate all the machinery on this vessel!"

McCoy had hurried out of the elevator. He rushed to the group, shouting, "Wait a minute!" He looked at the girl—and made his decision. "Miranda, I know you can do almost anything a sighted person can do—but you cannot pilot a Starship!"

She shrank back, stricken.

"What?" Kirk said.

"I'm sorry," McCoy said. "But the occasion calls for realism. You are blind, Miranda. And there are some things you just can't do."

Spock was eyeing the silvery embroidery on her sleeve. "Ah," he said. "A highly sophisticated sensor web. My compliments to your dressmaker, Dr. Jones."

The enigma unraveled for Kirk. She was safe with Kollos because she couldn't see him.

"I think I understand now," he said. "I know now why pity is the 'worst of all,' Miranda."

She flung her head high. "Pity which I do not deserve! Do you gather more information with your eyes than I do with my sensors? I could play tennis with you, Captain! I might even beat you. I am standing here exactly one meter and four centimeters from the door! Can you judge distance that accurately?"

"That won't be necessary," Kirk said gently. "Spock will make the mind-link. For your sake as well as ours."

"No! I won't let you do this!"

McCoy said, "I appeal to you as a colleague, Dr. Jones —don't fight us like this."

"No!"

"If none of us can persuade you, there is someone who can." Kirk used his command voice. "You will take this matter up with Ambassador Kollos."

She glared at him. Jerking open the cabin door, she entered and slammed it behind her.

Kirk eyed McCoy. "Why didn't you tell me, Bones?"

"She'd have told you herself if she'd wanted you to know. I respect her privacy."

"There's a great deal about this particular lady to resp—" Kirk stopped at the sound of a broken cry from the cabin. Unshamed tears streaming down her face, Miranda opened its door. McCoy started to her, but thinking better of it, waited for her to make the first move. It was to drag an arm across her tear-wet face. In the gesture was a childlike quality that went straight to Kirk's heart.

Still sobbing, she said, "It . . . seems that I have no choice . . . but to obey you."

The habitat had been removed to the bridge. A rigid metal screen hid it from all eyes but Spock's; and his were vizored. People barely breathed. Even the ship seemed to hold her breath. The sole sound was the quiet, majestic rhythm of Kollos's life support system. Alone with the black box behind the screen, Spock knelt and lifted the lid. The pure blue light flooded his face.

Hands pressed against the surface of the box, he leaned forward until his temples touched it. He backed away, gasping, eyes closed behind the vizor, his forehead beaded with sweat. A shudder shook him. Then, resolutely, he opened his eyes, inviting the light again.

Kirk's hands were wet. Still as cats, McCoy and Sulu waited. Chekov, at Spock's station, moved no buttons. Next to him, Uhura buried her face in her hands.

Somebody whispered, "Mr. Spock . . ."

Spock had stepped from behind the screen, pulling off the vizor. He looked relaxed, younger. And when he spoke, his voice was younger, warm and tender.

"How delightful to see you again!" he said. "I know you, all of you! James Kirk, my Captain and dear friend for years . . ."

He took a step toward Kirk, looking around him with interest. "And Leonard McCoy, another friend. And Uhura, whose name means freedom! Uhura who walks in beauty like the night . . ."

The shocked McCoy cried, "That can't be Spock!"

Cool and precise, Spock said, "Does it surprise you that I've read Byron, Doctor?"

"*That's* Spock!" McCoy said.

A mind-link to create a double entity. Those had been Spock's own words. "Am I . . . addressing the Medeusan Ambassador?" Kirk asked.

A radiant smile lit Spock's face. "In part—that is, that part of us that is known to you as Kollos. Where is Miranda? Ah, there you are! O, brave new world that boasts such beauty in it!"

She spoke harshly. "Tis new to thee, Mr. Spock."

His tone was that of a lover. "*My* world is next for you and me."

Kirk couldn't decipher the expression on her face, but she seemed to feel a need to hold herself under rigid control. But Spock's face was alive with such a naked tenderness that Kirk averted his eyes from it. The girl edged over to McCoy and Spock advanced to the command chair.

"Captain Kirk, I speak for all of us you call Medeusans.

I am sorry for the trouble I have brought to your ship."

"We can't hold you to blame for what happened, Ambassador. Thank you for helping us now."

The smile vanished. Spock was back, efficient, composed. "Now to the business at hand. With your permission, Captain?"

Kirk said, "Mr. Sulu, release the helm to Mr. Spock, please."

"Aye, sir."

At Sulu's console, Spock made rapid adjustments of switches. "Coordination is completed, Captain."

"Go ahead, then, Mr. Spock."

The engines began to throb again. "Warp factor one in six seconds," Spock said. "Five seconds . . ."

The ship was picking up speed. "Two seconds. One. Zero. . . ."

The searing light inundated the bridge. The great roar hammered. Bolt upright at the helm, Spock took the *Enterprise* back into its galaxy. "Position report, Mr. Chekov," he called.

Chekov's eyes were agog with admiration. "Bull's eye, Mr. Spock! Our position is so close to the point where we entered the void that the difference isn't worth mentioning!"

"That completes the maneuver, Captain," Spock said.

"Take over, Mr. Sulu."

As Spock vacated the helm, Kirk got to his feet. "Thank you, Ambassador. And now, Mr. Chekov, let's get her back on course."

Spock, flexing a hand, was intently examining it. The radiance shone in his face. "How compact your bodies are! And what a variety of senses you have! This thing you call language—it's most remarkable. You depend on it for so much. But is any of you really its master?" A look of infinite compassion came into his face. "But the aloneness. You are all so alone. How sad that you must live out your lives in this shell of flesh, contained and separate—how lonely you are, how lonely. . . ."

A warning bell sounded in Kirk's memory. The risk of the fusion was loss of separate identity. He turned in his chair. "Ambassador. It is time to dissolve the mind-link."

Who had answered him—Spock or Kollos? Kirk

couldn't tell. But the words seemed to come from a great distance.

"So soon?"

Kirk got to his feet. "You must not delay."

"You are wise, Captain."

With a debonair wave of the hand, Spock crossed to the metal screen, disappearing behind it. Miranda slipped after him to stand near the screen, her face concentrated, unreadable.

Uhura spoke. "Captain, Starfleet is calling."

"Audio, Lieutenant."

A radio voice cried, *"Enterprise!* Where have you people been?"

Behind the screen a kneeling Spock was bathed again in the pure blue radiance. As Kollos vacated his mind, he bowed his head under an oppressive sense of bereavement. He could hear Kirk saying, "Give them our position, Lieutenant. Tell them we'll send a full report later."

"Captain!"

The horror in Sulu's voice spun Kirk around to the helm station. Spock's forgotten vizor lay in Sulu's hand.

"Spock!" Kirk shouted. "Don't look! Cover your eyes!"

His cry was lost in the scream that came from behind the screen.

The shriek came again. Instinctively McCoy started toward the screen but was stopped dead in his tracks by Kirk's gesture of absolute command. "No! Don't move!"

"But, Jim . . ."

"No one is to move!" Kirk gave himself a moment to rally before he called, "Spock, are you all right?"

Time moved sluggish and slow. Kirk waited for the seconds to crawl by. Then Spock, backing out from behind the screen, turned his face to them. It was both terrified and terrifying—totally insane.

Kirk went to him, his hands outstretched. "It's all right now, Spock. You are safe with me."

But Spock had been transported to an unreachable realm. Lowering his head, he lunged at Kirk, aiming a fatal blow. Kirk ducked—and Spock, his madness distractible and purposeless, ripped out a lever from a console, hurling it across the bridge. Roaring like a wounded beast, he raged through the room, smashing at people and objects. Kirk found position for a straight phaser shot and stunned him at close range.

McCoy ran to the stilled body. Looking up, he cried, "He's hardly breathing, Jim! I must get him to Sickbay at once!"

Again time crawled by. Spock, insane, perhaps dying there before Kirk's eyes. As Marvick had died. Kirk covered his face with his hands to shut out the sight of the deathly white face on Sickbay's examination table. That brain of Spock's, whose magnificent resources had wrung victories out of countless defeats, deranged, lost to the *Enterprise,* lost to the friends who loved him. Behind his hands, Kirk could feel the skin of his face drawing into lines of haggard agony.

"Miranda," McCoy said. "Unless she reaches down into his mind and turns it outward to us, we will lose Spock, Jim."

Kirk could bear the sight of the world again. "Vulcan mind techniques!" Then his heart cringed. "She tried to help Marvick. She couldn't. He's dead."

"That was different. Marvick loved her."

Kirk paced restlessly. "Would she so much as try? Spock is her rival. He felt her jealousy of him."

"They were not rivals in love," McCoy said.

Kirk looked at him. "No. That's true. Bones, I'm taking action. Don't interfere with it. No matter what happens." He strode to the door of Sickbay and closed it behind him.

Miranda was in her cabin. And she knew what he'd come for. Telepathy, he thought grimly, had its advantages. It made explanation unnecessary. When she emerged from her bedroom, she was wearing a stark black tunic bare of the silver embroidery sensors. Truly blind now, she had to be guided to the door.

McCoy had had the examination table tilted almost upright. Spock's waxen, unmoving body was strapped to it. Kirk led Miranda over to it. "Your mind-link with him," he said. "It must bring him back from wherever he is."

Nearly as pale as Spock, she said, "You must leave us alone, Captain."

At his desk McCoy didn't speak. Once more Kirk

waited. If the memories of Spock's loyal valor would only stop returning . . . but they wouldn't stop. And what was going on in that examination room? Spock had spoken of her "thirst for power."

Kirk walked into the examination room.

She looked up at the sound of the opening door. "Dr. McCoy?"

"It's I, the Captain."

"I have no news for you." She paused. "His life processes are failing."

The blue, blind eyes had groped for his. Kirk steeled himself against a wave of compassion for her. "And what are you doing about it?"

"Why . . . what I can, of course."

"It doesn't seem to be much!"

It sparked a flash of anger from her. "No doubt you expect me to wake up your Sleeping Beauty with a kiss!"

The compassion died in him. "It might be worth trying," he told her. "He's not a machine."

"He is a Vulcan!" she cried.

"Half of him. The other half is human—a half more human than you seem to be!"

She faced him, rage working in her face. "Face reality, Captain Kirk. His mind has gone too deep even for me to reach."

"And if you don't reach it, he will die. Isn't that what you want?"

She stared at him wordlessly, her mouth open. Then, in a small, unbelieving voice, she said, "Why . . . that is a lie!"

"You want him to die," Kirk said.

He caught her by the arm. "What did you do on the bridge? Did you make him forget to vizor his eyes?"

She wrenched her arm free. *"You* are insane."

He seized it again, his jaw hard. "You know your rival! He made a mind-link with Kollos—exactly what you have never been able to do!"

She struck at him, beating at his face with her fists. He immobilized her hands, holding her tight within the hard circle of his arms. "With my words," he said, "I will make you hear the ugliness Spock saw when his naked eyes looked at Kollos! Ugliness is deep in you, Miranda!"

"Liar! Liar! Liar!" she screamed.

"Listen to me. Your passion to see Kollos is madness. You are blind. You can never see him. Never! But Spock has seen him. And for that he must die. That's it, isn't it?"

She twisted in his arms. "Sadistic, filthy liar . . ."

"You smell of hatred. The stench of jealousy fills you. Why don't you strangle him as he lies there, helpless?"

Strength drained out of her. "No . . . no . . . don't say any more, please."

"Kollos knows what is in your heart. You can lie to yourself—but you can't lie to Kollos."

"Go away! Please . . . go away."

Kirk released her. She staggered but he reached no hand to help her. The door closed behind him.

In his office McCoy got up from his desk. Kirk sank into his chair and, leaning his arms on the desk, rested his head on them, shaken, exhausted.

"Are you all right?" McCoy asked.

Kirk didn't answer. McCoy laid a hand on the bowed shoulders. "What did you say to her, Jim?"

Kirk lifted his head. "Maybe too much."

"What is she doing in there? If she can't—"

"Maybe I shouldn't have gone in, Bones."

"Jim . . ."

"I went at her in the dark. In her darkness. In her blindness. If he dies. . . ."

"Don't, Jim."

"If he dies, how do I know I didn't kill him? How can I know she can stand to hear the truth?"

In the room behind them, she had moved to Spock, her fingers probing at his temples. In a whisper choked with fury, she was saying, "This is to the death—or life for both of us. Do you hear me, Spock?"

He was in a cavern, his eyes open. Over him hovered a Miranda, her hair a writhing nest of snakes. They hissed at him, their fangs dripping venom. He let it drip on his face. The Miranda laughed demoniacally. The venom stung. Then there were three Mirandas, chuckling with pleasure in his pain. When he put his hands over his ears to shut out the hideous chuckles, there were seven Mirandas. He groveled on his knees, clutching at his ears. The laughing stopped.

But the Fury wasn't finished with him. The cavern was a pool. A Miranda had him by the throat. She was very strong and he was tired. The water of the pool closed over his head. She pushed it down . . . down. His hands felt heavy, clumsy, strangely disobedient. But at last they did his bidding and tore her grasp from his throat. The water still dragged at him. Then his soul moved. He stumbled out of the water's hold; and in a curious unsurprise, realized that the Miranda was helping him. He coughed frothy water from his lungs, and dreamily heard the Miranda say, "So you have decided to live after all. But there is one thing more—the madness. . . ."

A box lid was open, radiating a blue light he seemed to remember. He was about to look into the half-familiar box when its lid dropped.

He was very tired. There was a door in front of him. On a last spurt of strength, he opened it.

"Spock!"

It was the voice of his dear Captain.

Spock staggered to him. In his flood of returning sanity, he recognized McCoy. But as usual the Doctor was fussing. "You have no business to be out of bed! Sit here!"

He sat. His Captain left him to go somewhere else, calling, "Miranda!"

But if there had ever been a Miranda around, she was gone.

With meticulous care Spock placed Kollos's habitat on the Transporter platform. His hands lingered on the box—a final communion. Kirk looked at the hands, his eyes warm with affection. Pointing to Spock, he smiled at the woman beside him. "I have you to thank for his life," he said.

He spoke to a different Miranda—one transfigured by the same wondering innocence that had entered into Spock during his mind-link with Kollos. McCoy, moved by the new purity of her lovely face, said, "You now have what you wanted most, Miranda?"

"Yes. I am one with Kollos."

McCoy took her hand and kissed it. "I am truly sorry that you are leaving us."

She stepped back to Kirk. "We have come to the end of an eventful trip, Captain."

"I wasn't sure you'd even speak to me."

The blue radiance of the box was in her blue eyes. "I have you to thank for my future. What you said has enabled me to *see*. I shall not need my sensors any more."

He lifted a white rose from the Transporter console. "My good-bye gift to you," he said.

The rose against her cheek, she said, "I suppose it has thorns, Captain."

"I never met a rose that didn't, Miranda."

At the platform, Spock, in dress uniform, was wearing his IDIC. The girl touched it. "I understand the symbology, now, Mr. Spock. The marvel is in the infinite diversity of life."

He met her eyes gravely. "And in the ways our differences can combine to create new truth and beauty."

She took her position on the platform as Spock adjusted his vizor for the last time. Then he lifted his hand in the Vulcan salute.

She returned it. "Peace and long life to you, Mr. Spock," she said.

"Peace and long life, Miranda."

At the Transporter console, Kirk himself moved the dematerializing switches.

A PRIVATE LITTLE WAR

(Don Ingalls and Gene Roddenberry)

McCoy stretched his back muscles, tired from bending over his collection of soil, leaves and roots. Starfleet had something, he thought. This planet's plant culture just might be a medical El Dorado. But he was glad when his communicator beeped. This clearing in the forest was lonely.

Kirk said, "How much longer, Bones?"

"About another thirty minutes, Jim. You and Spock find anything?"

"No sign of inhabitants so far. Continue collecting. Kirk out." As he closed his communicator, Spock pointed to the scuffled stones on the rocky ledge where they stood. "The apelike carnivore of the reports, Captain?"

Kirk inspected the tracks. He straightened, nodding. "The gumato. But this spoor is several days old. No problem. They seldom stay in one place."

Spock eyed the sweep of trees sloping downhill from their ledge. "Aside from that, you say it's a Garden of Eden, sir?"

Kirk grinned. "So it seemed years ago to a brash young Lieutenant named Kirk in command of his first planet survey." He stiffened, hearing a branch break. Then he saw the people below moving along a narrow trail cut through the trees. With a shock of pleasure, he recognized their leader; and was about to shout "Tyree!" when his eye caught the glint of sun on a gun barrel. Guns—on this planet! He seized his phaser and Spock said quietly, "Use of our weapons was expressly forbidden, Captain."

"Tyree is leading those people into ambush! He's the friend I lived with here!" He wheeled; and kicking hard at a rock outcropping, loosed it to send it careening down the slope. The ambusher's exploded from their concealing underbrush and Tyree cried, *"Villagers!"*

His group broke, rushing for the trees' shelter. But one of the ambushers, turning, had seen Kirk and Spock. He yelled something to the other two; and all three ambushers burst into a fast run up the hill toward the *Enterprise* men. Then the first paused to place a flintlock musket against his shoulder. The bullet *pinged* past Kirk's ear to strike spray from the rock behind him. The man pulled up to reload—and the second villager fired. Hot metal tore into Spock.

In his clearing McCoy heard the shots. Snatching his communicator, he opened it, crying, *"Enterprise,* alert! Alert! Stand by to beam up landing party!"

Spock was down. Running to him, Kirk took one look at the wound; and grabbing his phaser, aimed it at their pursuers.

"No . . . Captain . . ."

"Spock, they'll be reloaded in a moment!"

On a surge of agonized effort, Spock staggered to his feet. "No, I . . . can travel."

Looking up, Kirk saw McCoy and cried, "Beam us up fast, Bones!" McCoy had his communicator open. *"Now,* Scotty! Spock's hurt! Have medics standing by!"

Kirk, supporting the half-conscious Spock, pulled him into a threesome with McCoy. As they dematerialized, the three villagers were left to stare at the sparkle into which they'd disappeared.

An agitated Scott was at the Transporter platform to meet them. "What happened, Captain?"

"Lead projectile. Old-style firearm. Tell those medics to bring the stretcher closer!"

As the reeling Spock was eased onto it, Nurse Chapel and Doctor M'Benga hurried into the Transporter Room. McCoy, his eyes on Spock's torn chest, said, "Vitalizer B." Christine Chapel swiftly adjusted a hypo and McCoy pressed it, hissing, against Spock's limp arm. It was as she reached into her medikit that Spock subsided into unconsciousness. M'Benga, his medical scanner humming, passed it over the motionless body.

Christine spoke to McCoy. "Pressure packet ready, Doctor."

He took it; and lifting Spock's shirt, pushed it into the wound. "Lucky his heart's where his liver should be—or he'd be dead now." It wasn't a joke. His face was grim. "Set hypo for coradrenalin."

As the syringe hissed again, Kirk spoke. "Bones, you can save him, can't you?"

Without warning, alarm sirens shrieked. Sinister red lights flashed and Uhura's filtered voice said, *"All decks, red alert! Battle stations! This is no drill. Battle stations! Red alert!"*

Kirk leaped to the intercom. "Bridge, this is the Captain."

"Lieutenant Uhura, sir. We have a Klingon vessel on our screens."

"On my way!"

He was at the door when he brought up short. Looking back to where McCoy was working over Spock, he said, "Bones . . ."

"I don't know, Jim!"

Choices. Kirk opened the door to a corridor, hideous with the screech of sirens. They were screaming on the bridge, too. Chekov had taken Spock's position at the library computer; and Uhura, motionless at her board, was listening intently. Chekov looked up as Kirk, Scott on his heels, ran from the elevator. "No change of position, sir. They may not have seen us. We're holding the planet between us and the Klingon."

Uhura moved in her chair. "Make that definite. They're sending a routine message to their home base. No mention of us, sir."

"Then reduce to alert one, Lieutenant."

She hit her intercom button. "All stations, go to yellow alert. Repeat, cancel battle stations. Remain on yellow alert."

The sirens stilled. Kirk crossed to the helm, checked it; and turned to look at the viewing screen. All it held was the image of the planet.

"Think you can keep us out of their sight, Scotty?"

Scott moved a control on the helm. "I can try, sir."

He spoke to Chekov. "Lock scanners into astrogation circuits."

"Locking in, sir."

"Message to Starbase, Captain?" Uhura asked.

Kirk shook his head. "No point in giving ourselves away, Lieutenant. Not until we find out what's going on."

"We can hide for a while, Captain." Scott had turned from the helm. "But we may have to leave orbit to keep it up long."

Kirk nodded. He went to his command position to hit the intercom button on his panel. "Captain to Sickbay."

"McCoy here. I'll call you as soon as I know anything. I don't now. Sickbay out."

So that was that. As they say, time would tell. Time alone would tell whether Spock would survive to live another day—or whether he wouldn't. Kirk struggled against an upsurge of panic. It wouldn't do. Another subject—one to take the mind off Spock's peril. He turned to Scott.

"That Klingon is breaking the treaty," he said.

"Not necessarily, sir. They've as much right to scientific missions here as we have."

"Research is hardly the Klingon preoccupation."

"True, Captain. But since that's a 'hands off' planet, you can't prove they're up to anything else."

Kirk frowned. "When I left that planet seventeen years ago, the villagers down there had barely learned to forge iron into crude plows. But Spock was shot by a flintlock. How many centuries between those two developments?"

Uhura answered. "On Earth about twelve centuries, sir."

"On the other hand," Scott said, "a flintlock would be the first type firearm the inhabitants would normally develop."

Kirk snapped, "I'm aware of that, Mr. Scott."

Chekov spoke. "And, sir, the fact that Earth took twelve centuries doesn't mean they have to."

Over at her board Uhura nodded. "We've seen development at different rates on different planets."

"If it were the Klingons behind this, why didn't they give them breechloaders?" Scott asked. "Or machine guns? Or early hand lasers or—"

A PRIVATE LITTLE WAR

Kirk interrupted, angry. "I made a simple comment. I didn't invite a debate."

But Scott didn't waver. "Captain, you made a *number* of comments. And you've always insisted that we give you honest reactions. If that's changed, sir . . ."

"It hasn't," Kirk said. He swung his chair around. "I'm sorry. I'm worried about Spock. And I'm concerned about something that's happened to what I once knew down there." He got up and made for the elevator. "You have the con, Scotty. I'll be waiting in Sickbay."

He could feel the controlled tension in Sickbay the moment he entered it. McCoy, Doctor M'Benga and Christine were all gathered around Spock's still-unconscious form. The sterilite above it swathed it in its eerie glow. Kirk glanced up at the body-functions panel. Its readings were ominously low. There was, of course, the factor of Spock's different Vulcan physiology. But Christine was looking very troubled. And Spock might have been dead, so lifeless he looked on the table.

M'Benga spoke. "We've no replacements for the damaged organs, Doctor. If he's going to heal, his Vulcan physiology will have to do it for him."

"Agreed," McCoy said. "Sterilite off." He moved to his office. Kirk followed him. They eyed each other for a long moment. Then McCoy said, "He may live. He may die. I don't know which."

Kirk paced the distance to the door and back to McCoy's desk. McCoy gestured to the exam room. "Doctor M'Benga interned in a Vulcan hospital, Jim. Spock couldn't be in better hands."

"You're sure of that?"

"Yes."

Kirk hesitated. Then he came to his hard decision. "All right. You and I are transporting back down to the planet, Bones."

"I can't leave Spock at such a time."

"You just indicated you could." He leaned his hands on McCoy's desk. "There are Klingons down there. If their mission is a legitimate research interest in the planet's organic potential, you're the one man who can tell me."

"And if that's not it?"

"Then I'll need help." He pointed to the exam room. "I'll need advice I can trust as much as I trust Spock's."

"That's a rare compliment, Jim, but—"

Kirk flared. "Blast it, McCoy, I'm worried about Spock, too! But if the Klingons are breaking the 'hands off' treaty here, there could be an interstellar war at stake!" He strode to the office intercom. Hitting the button, he said, "Captain to bridge."

"Scott here, sir."

"McCoy and I are beaming back down. Inform ship's stores we'll need native costumes."

"Captain, I may have to break orbit any minute to keep out of their sight. We'd be out of communication range with you."

Kirk was thinking fast. The secrecy of their presence was vital. Any attempt to contact Starfleet Command could reveal it. Asking permission to violate orders concerning this "hands off" planet was a risk he dare not take. He'd have to act alone, on his own judgment.

He turned back to the intercom. "I understand, Scotty. We'll set up a rendezvous schedule. Captain out."

They materialized near a copse of trees. Glancing around, Kirk got his bearings. The copse dipped to a rocky glade he remembered. Tyree's camp was about a quarter of a mile distant.

McCoy, tricorder out, said, "Want to think about this again, Jim? Starfleet's orders are no interference with this planet's state."

" 'With its normal social development.' I'm not only aware of the orders, Bones. It was my survey seventeen years ago that recommended them."

McCoy nodded. "I read your report. 'Inhabitants superior in many ways to humans. Left alone, they will undoubtedly someday develop a remarkably advanced and peaceful culture.' "

"And I intend to see that they get their chance. Are you coming with me, Doctor?"

They moved off down the shale of the glade. The terrain ahead showed bigger rocks and a thick growth of underbrush. McCoy was still troubled; but Kirk, recognizing familiar landmarks, was buoyant. He gestured to some foliage. "The saplings over there, they make good bows. We used to choose our wood from this very spot."

"Almost like coming home, eh?"

"It'll be good to see Tyree again. During that year here, we were made brothers. I lived with his family, wore his Hillpeople clothes. We hunted together...."

McCoy halted abruptly. "All right, Jim. I'll try just once more."

Kirk turned, his eyes questioning. McCoy's met them unflinchingly. "So you love this place. Fine! So you want to see an old friend again. Also fine! You believe the Klingons are here, threatening all that you admire so much."

"Bones, we've been over this—"

"You asked me to replace Spock's advice and judgment! Well, I'm doing the best I can to!" There was a deep, sincere concern in McCoy's face. "Jim, I admire a Starship Captain willing to disobey orders—and risk his career when necessary. But how much of this decision of yours is emotion . . . and how much of it is logic?"

Kirk's mouth moved in a small smile. "Logic? I suppose Spock *would* ask that." He pondered the question. "I *do* have an emotional attachment to this place. That's obvious. However—"

McCoy interrupted again. "Spock might also suggest that for twenty-four hours we reconnoiter—and obey orders, making no contacts. If you decide to move in after that, I'm with you."

Kirk looked at the earnest eyes. "All right, Bones. We stay out of sight for a day. We'll cut through here and—"

He never finished his sentence. There was a hoarse snarl—and a huge, hairy creature, faintly gorillalike, lips crawled back over its wicked teeth, burst out of a clump of brush where it had been hiding. A clawed fist the size of a ham knocked Kirk from his feet. Then it leaped for McCoy in the very act of reaching for his phaser. He was slammed back into rock, the weapon knocked from his hand. He fell, stunned—and the aroused gumato turned on Kirk again. He went down once more, the beast's frothy jaws tearing at the flesh of his shoulder. McCoy, trying frantically to clear his head, stretched an arm toward his phaser. Kirk landed a hard kick in the animal's belly; but the fury of the alien thing clawed him down. McCoy grasped his phaser; and making a swift adjustment on it, shouted, "Jim . . . roll free so I can shoot!"

He fired a stun charge. The gumato staggered. Then it whirled on McCoy, roaring. He got to his knees, loosing the full phaser power. The gumato vanished. But Kirk lay still. McCoy crawled to him, medikit out.

"Contact ship," Kirk whispered. "I took . . . full poison . . . its fangs. . . ."

The hypo hissed against his arm. Then McCoy spoke into his communicator. "Landing party to *Enterprise*, come in! *Enterprise, this is McCoy! Emergency! Come in!*"

Kirk's forehead was already beading with sweat. The poison was in his bloodstream. McCoy had to stoop to hear the weakening voice. "Afraid . . . they've left . . . orbit."

"Jim, there's no antitoxin for this." He used the hypo again. "I can keep you alive for only a few hours with these injections."

"Tyree . . . some of them have . . . cure."

Kirk slumped into unconsciousness. In the lonely silence, McCoy heard a twig snap. Three men, bows and spears at the ready, were standing behind him, suspicion and curiosity equally mingled in their faces.

"Are you Hillpeople? Do you know a hunter named Tyree?" McCoy gestured to Kirk. "A gumato attacked him. He's James Kirk, a friend of Tyree. . . ." He waited for some response. None came. *"Blast it, do something!"* he shouted. *"He's dying!"*

But the Hillpeople still stared at him stolidly.

Later, he was to feel grateful to them. Their settlement was crude, even for a nomadic people—a place of firepits, log shelters and primitive pottery. But the cave into which they carried Kirk's limp body was warm. And the pallet they laid him on was soft with animal skins. He was wet now with sweat and beginning to tremble violently. McCoy turned to the man who had directed them into the cave. "Yutan, more skins—blankets. I must keep him warm."

When the coverings came, McCoy piled them on Kirk.

Tyree's woman—she was said to possess a cure for the effects of gumato venom. But both were absent from the camp. Superstition, anyway. And yet . . . there was Starfleet's extraordinary interest in the medical promise of this planet's organic substances. . . .

Kirk was babbling in the first stages of delirium. It would reach its climax. Then coma and death. McCoy looked desperately around the cave. Slowly he got to his feet. Incredibly the boulder opposite him moved when he pushed it. Straining against its weight, he rolled it over beside Kirk. After a moment he went toward another one. "You and your 'Garden of Eden,'" he muttered. "First Spock, now you. Maybe Adam was better off out of Eden."

Tyree and his woman were crouched in the shadow of a rocky overhang, watching a file of villagers pass down a trail, armed with their flintlocks. Though the woman's wild black hair had never known a comb, her thin features held intelligence and a savage beauty. She leaned to Tyree, whispering urgently. "We must obtain the same firesticks, husband! We could take their goods, their horses—kill them!"

"Enough!" he rebuked. "In time the villagers will return to the ways of friendship."

She spotted a small plant beside her. Its root came up to the prize of her sharp-bladed knife. "In time?" she said. "How many of us must continue to die waiting for this 'time' of yours?"

Tyree opened her small leather bag for her. As she dropped the root into it, she said, "I am a *Kahn-ut-tu* woman, Tyree! In all this land there are few of us. Men seek us for mates because through us they can become great leaders!"

He smiled at her. "I took you for mate because you cast a spell upon me, Nona."

She withdrew an odd-shaped leaf from her bag. The look in her brilliant dark eyes was openly inviting. "And I have spells to keep you!" She crushed the leaf until its heady scent had impregnated her fingers. "Remember this fragrance? The night we camped by the water . . . ?"

He pushed her away. "Yes. The night of madness."

She caressed his face with her scented fingers. His eyelids drooped. She leaned closer to him. "Madness? Did you really hate *that* madness, Tyree?"

"No," he pleaded. "Nona, no. It calls up evil beasts from my soul."

"Only one lovely beast, Tyree . . . you, my strong, angry man."

His arms went around her. He was drawing her down to the leaves when Yutan, running, broke through the trees. Nona looked up; and he stopped dead at the look in her eyes.

"For . . . forgive me," he stammered. "But there are strangers in the camp. One has taken a gumato bite. He dies."

Nona was on her feet. "Strangers? Explain."

"It is said that the dying one is a friend of Tyree. From long ago."

Tyree was still fighting the intoxicating effects of the leaf's odor; but Nona, in full command of herself, nodded. "That one!" she exclaimed. "I go. Bring Tyree when his head clears."

Kirk was moaning in the clutch of his delirium. McCoy went to the cave entrance. The curious crowd that had thronged it had disappeared. He pulled his phaser, aimed it at one of the boulders beside Kirk, and fired it. The rock glowed red with heat. With perhaps too much. He bent over the phaser to readjust it—and Nona, a dark ghost, slipped into the cave. She looked from the red rock to the weapon in McCoy's hands, her face alive with fascinated interest. Pulling back into the shadows, she watched the phaser beam strike the other boulder. It, too, went red. Nona turned and left the cave as silently as she'd entered it.

Tyree, Yutan beside him, was running toward it. She extended a hand. "Stop!" she said. "Do you want me to save him?"

Her tone halted him. "You must!" he cried. "He is the one I told you of, the friend of my young days!"

She had seen a miracle—a firestick of marvelous power. A *Kahn-ut-tu* woman knew how to take advantage of miraculous opportunities. Wife to a supreme leader of men . . .

"My remedies," she said, "require full knowledge of the people they cure. I must know all that is known of your friend."

Tyree shook his head. "I gave him the Promise of Silence, Nona. He was made my *brother!*"

"And I am your wife—his sister. I promise silence also. *Quickly,* Tyree. Or he dies!"

Spock had still to recover consciousness. Christine Chapel, frightened, looked away from the low readings on his body-functions panel. Maybe his pulse . . . She took it and her hand slipped down to hold his. Words she didn't know were in her came to her lips. "Mr. Spock, you've hardly ever noticed me . . . and I understand. You can't. But—I'd give my life to save you. . . ."

Sickbay's door opened. She hurriedly replaced Spock's arm on the bed—but M'Benga had seen.

He examined the panel. "Don't let those readings unduly trouble you. I've seen this before in Vulcans. It's their way of concentrating their strength, blood and antibodies on the injured organs." He eyed the pale face on the pillow. "A form of self-induced hypnosis."

"You mean he's actually conscious, Doctor?"

"In a sense. He knows we're here and what we're saying. But he can't take his mind from the tissue he is fighting to heal. I suppose," he added, "that he even knows you were holding his hand."

He left her, eyes averted from the painful flush that flooded her face. She moved to gather up some charts. Then she turned to address the still form on the bed. "Mr. Spock," she said, "a good nurse holds the hands of all patients. It proves to them that one is . . . interested."

The lie made her feel much better.

The boulders were cooling. But it was still very hot in the cave. McCoy brushed sweat from his face and bent to pull back Kirk's eyelid. He shook his head; and was drawing a blanket closer about him when Tyree and Nona walked into the cave.

The man spoke at once. "I am Tyree." He strode to Kirk as one who had the right, passing the dull red rocks without a glance. But McCoy's interest was focused on

Nona. She was emptying the contents of a small leather bag on a flat rock. He moved in to watch her over her shoulder. "And I am Tyree's woman," she told him without turning.

On the rock's flat surface lay a root, wet, covered with small open spores. Nona drew her razor-edged knife, pressed its blade on the root—and it began to writhe. She picked it up on the flat of her knife, speaking briefly. "A Mahko root."

"A plant?" said the wary McCoy. "It moves."

"For one who knows where to find it and how to pick it."

Tyree was kneeling at Kirk's head, his kindly face anxious. When Nona approached them, he pulled back so that she could seat herself next to his friend, the root still moving on the knife blade. When she touched Kirk's throat with her free hand, his mouth opened slightly. She leaned over him gently; and exhaling a long breath of her own between his lips, whispered, "Take this of my soul ... this of my soul into thy soul ... into thine...."

McCoy was shocked. He turned to Tyree, crying, "I was told she had a *cure!*"

"Be silent," he said sternly.

Nona was breathing more of her breath into Kirk's open mouth. She lifted unseeing eyes, chanting more of her strange incantation. "Deeply ... deeply ... deeply ... we must become as one ... as one ... as one...."

To McCoy's total amazement, Kirk had begun to breathe evenly in time with the woman's breathing. But the mystic element in the chant horrified him. He had started toward Kirk when Tyree's strong arm barred the way. He saw Nona bare the exact spot on Kirk's shoulder where the gumato fangs had struck, and slap the twisting root on the punctures. Then, turning the knife on her own hand, she slashed it deeply and pressed it, bleeding, on top of the ugly root. She groaned with pain. Kirk echoed the groan as though he, too, felt the agony of the slash. She shut her eyes. Swaying, she chanted, "Together ... your pain in mine ... together ... your soul in mine ... together ... together ... together...."

Both of them were now inhaling in perfect unison. And

to both, in unison, came easier breath, relaxation. Nona's eyes fluttered open. "Return . . . it is past . . . return . . . return . . . return. . . ."

And Kirk's eyes, too, fluttered open. Against the animal skins of his pallet, his face was at peace.

Nona remained close to him for a long moment. Then very slowly she withdrew her hand from his shoulder. She extended it, palm up, to McCoy. It held no sign of knife wound, only the small, withered thing that had been the writhing root. She got to her feet, making way for McCoy. But he didn't need to examine Kirk's shoulder. He knew what he'd find—and he found it. The flesh was healthy, unmarked.

Kirk smiled up at him. "I've been having . . . a strange dream."

"How do you feel, Jim?"

"I'm tired—just tired. You've done a fine job, Bones."

He was already asleep. McCoy looked up to see Tyree supporting Nona.

"Thank you for saving him. I'd like to learn more of this. . . ."

"She must sleep now," Tyree said.

"Is there any condition I should watch for in him? Any aftereffect or danger?"

Nona spoke weakly. "Our blood has passed . . . through the Mahko root together . . . our souls have been together. He is mine now."

Startled, McCoy spoke to Tyree. "What does she mean, 'he's hers'?"

"When a man and a woman are joined in this manner, he can refuse her no wish." He smiled faintly. "But only a legend. There is no danger."

Tyree was leading her from the cave when she passed close to McCoy. Though her eyes were heavy with exhaustion, there was a look on her face that troubled McCoy. It suggested that she knew she had won some obscure victory. When he noted the same half-smile of satisfaction on Kirk's sleeping features, McCoy's sense of apprehension became definite.

It grew so insistent it aroused him from his deep sleep of weariness. The cave was black with night. His first conscious thought was of Kirk. He reached for his medikit and groped his way past the rocks to the pallet. It was empty.

He stood still for a moment, fully awake now. The layout of the camp was still unfamiliar to him. He moved to the cave entrance, trying to get his bearings in the darkness. To his left there was the darker shadow of a structure of some kind. It turned out to be a lean-to. The still-glowing embers of its firepit showed two sleepers. A dim form was standing over one of them.

"Jim?" McCoy whispered.

One of the sleepers awoke, rolling instantly into a crouch. It was Tyree. He stared at McCoy. Then, bounding to his feet, he turned and saw Kirk, eyes closed like a sleepwalker's, beside the sleeping body of his wife.

"Jim!" McCoy shook Kirk's arm. The eyes opened to fill with surprise. "Quite . . . all right, Bones. I felt better and thought I'd stretch my legs." He recognized Tyree; his face alight with pleasure, cried, *"Tyree! It is you, my old friend!"* His hand went out to grip the man's shoulder in genuine affection.

Nona had awakened. Tyree gave her a quick glance. There was a pause before he said, "Yes, James. It is good to see you."

"But what am I doing here? How did . . . ? No, I remember now. A gumato bite. I was ill. . . ." He gestured to McCoy. "I told the Doctor here, 'take me to Tyree's camp.' I knew you'd find a *Kahn-ut-tu* to cure me." He turned to McCoy. "The *Kahn-ut-tus* are a kind of local witch people . . . actually healers who have studied the herbs and roots here."

"And I am a *Kahn-ut-tu* woman, Captain." Nona smiled at Kirk. "I cured you."

Their eyes met; and Tyree said, "My woman. Nona."

In the light of the firepit's embers, the wild, disheveled black hair enhanced the savage beauty of her face. "Yes, of course," Kirk said. "Your woman."

McCoy spoke. "Tyree leads the Hillpeople here."

Kirk smiled at his friend. "Congratulations—on both counts."

"You need rest, Jim."

"Rest? I've never felt more alive!" Kirk's face sobered.

A PRIVATE LITTLE WAR

"Tyree, can we talk now? The villagers' new weapons. I want to hear all about that. We have plans to make."

Nona broke in. "Good. It is past time to plan."

Tyree nodded. "Yes, much has happened since you left. Come, we will speak of it—"

"And of things to be done!" said Nona.

Tyree looked at her. Then silently, he led the way out of the lean-to.

Spock lay as pale, as motionless as ever.

Doctor M'Benga, entering Sickbay, nodded to Christine; and going to Spock, leaned close to a pointed ear. He spoke very slowly and distinctly. "This is Doctor M'Benga, Mr. Spock. There'll be someone with you constantly from now on. When the time comes, I'll be called." He straightened. "Nurse, stay with him."

Christine had her eyes on the body-functions panel. "The readings are beginning to fluctuate markedly, Doctor."

"So they should be," M'Benga said. "The moment he shows any sign of consciousness, call me immediately."

"Yes, Doctor."

He was making for the door when he turned. "After you have called me, if he speaks, do whatever he says."

"Whatever he says?"

"Yes, that's clear enough, isn't it?"

It was clear. It was also disconcerting. She looked at the pointed ears on the pillow. They suddenly struck her as extremely aristocratic.

Tyree was making good on his promise to bring Kirk up to date on the firearms question. "It's less than a year ago that their firesticks first came to the villagers. Since that time, my friend, almost one in three of us have died."

Kirk leaned forward over the rude table. "But you say they make the firesticks themselves? You can't be certain of that."

"We've looked into their village and saw it being done."

"Tyree," McCoy said, "have you seen strangers among the villagers?"

Tyree shook his head, "Never."

Behind them, unseen, Nona had slipped into the hut to immerse herself in the shadows of a corner. She watched McCoy turn to Kirk. "Meanwhile," he said, "you have made contact here. If it turns out that we are the ones who broke the 'hands off' treaty, it's your career, Jim."

"Perhaps, Bones. But it would hardly take a platoon of Klingons to teach them to make crude firearms."

"A single one would be too slow and inefficient if they really want this planet."

"But much more *clever*," Kirk said. "If they'd armed them with Klingon lasers or even repeating rifles, it would be obvious they'd interfered here." He spoke to Tyree. "Can you get us to their main village while it's still dark?"

Tyree hesitated. "The gumatos travel at night also. If you killed one, its mate will not leave."

Kirk laid his phaser on the table. "You've seen these work. So long as no one else sees them used—"

Nona stepped forward into the light of their pitch torch. "I also have seen them used."

Kirk swiftly replaced his phaser. Nona had turned to McCoy. "I saw you heat those stones with yours." Her eyes sought Kirk's. "And I know you have many ways to make Tyree a man of great importance."

McCoy eyed her. "Many ways?" He spoke to Tyree. "What else does she know about us?"

"Tyree has told me much of you." She smiled at Kirk. "Do not blame him. It was the price for saving your life."

McCoy slammed the table. "Demonstrating the wisdom of Starfleet orders!" he cried. "First, there's contact made . . . then a mistake, an accident. It has to be set right by a small intervention with natural evolution. The correction goes wrong—and more intervention is necessary. . . ."

Kirk had reddened with anger. *"Thank you, Doctor!"* He spoke to Nona. "We are simply strangers from—"

"From one of the lights in the sky!" She nodded. "I know. And you have ways as far above firesticks as the sky is above our world!"

Tyree half-rose to his feet. "You will not speak of that to others!"

She ignored him to address Kirk. "I will not if I am made to understand. Teach me." She paused. "There's an old custom among my people. When a woman saves a man's life, he is grateful."

McCoy, eyes narrowed, watched Kirk. He waited—and Kirk said, "I am grateful."

"Highly commendable," McCoy said dryly. "If not carried to extremes."

But Kirk was waving Nona to a seat. It was clear that he was making a conscious effort to choose words cautiously. "We were once as you are, Nona. Spears and arrows. Then came the time when our weapons grew faster than our wisdom. We almost killed ourselves. So we made a rule. It said that we must never cause the same thing to happen to other worlds we visited. Do you understand?"

She didn't answer. Kirk laid a hand on Tyree's arm. "As a man must grow in his own way and in his own time, so must worlds. They—"

She interrupted. "Some men never grow."

"Perhaps not as fast or in the way another thinks he should. But we are now wise enough to know how unwise it is to interfere with the way of another man or another world."

"You will let the villagers destroy us? You will not help your friend and brother to kill them instead?"

Tyree sprang to his feet. "I have said I will not kill, woman! There are better ways!"

Her eyes flashed dark fire. "We must fight or die! Is dying better?" She whirled to Kirk. "You would let him die when you have weapons to make him powerful and safe? Then he has the wrong friends—and I have the wrong man!" She rushed from the hut.

Tyree made no move to follow her. After an awkward pause, he said, "You will help in ways she does not understand. I have faith in our friendship, friend. Come —or we lose the darkness."

As he left, McCoy saw the pained look on Kirk's face. "What's bothering you? If we find the Klingons have armed the villagers, we can certainly do something about that."

Kirk rose. "That's what bothers me—the 'something' we may have to do."

They found Tyree waiting at the camp's edge. Despite the night, he was unhesitating as he led them along the trail winding downward to the village. The trees thinned—and he lifted a warning finger. A guard, flintlock at shoulder, was pacing his rounds on the village outskirts. The three came to a halt behind the bole of a massive tree.

"We'll wait for the guard to circle back." Kirk leaned back against the tree. "You have quite a wife, Tyree. Beautiful *and* intelligent."

Tyree gave him a quick look; and seeing the sincerity in his face, nodded. "A *Kahn-ut-tu* woman is always a prize. They have . . . ways of making a man happy."

"I remember the stories about them."

"But mine talks too much of killing."

"An ambitious woman is a treasure," McCoy said. "Or a time bomb."

Kirk spoke slowly. "Tyree, suppose . . . you *had* to fight? Suppose it were the only way?"

"Jim! This man believes the very thing we believe—killing is useless and stupid! What kind of question is that?"

Again Kirk was abruptly aware of loneliness—the loneliness of the immense responsibility he had chosen to undertake. Well, he'd taken it. For better or worse, it had to be borne now. He was in this thing up to his neck. He straightened. The guard was returning. He slid away from the tree bole to slip through the night, weaving his way from shadow to shadow. When the guard was within a foot of him, he downed him with a karate chop. Then, seizing the gun, he passed it to Tyree, saying, "Keep this. Wait for us."

The village's buildings were more sophisticated than the simple constructions of Tyree's camp. Some were lighted. Kirk and McCoy, keeping to shadows, saw a man approaching one of the larger ones. What they could glimpse of his thinly bearded face seemed to be that of some scholarly ascetic; but in the light of the opening door, it showed up crafty, even malignant. Circling the house, they found a window; and huddled under it, watched him cross a room to a map-covered table. Sitting at it, a new flintlock beside him, was another man, his back turned to them. But Kirk didn't have to see the cruel, lipless Klingon face. He had recognized the tailored metallic Klingon dress. And a Klingon weapon hung at its belt.

"You are late, Apella," the Klingon said.

"A quarrel to be judged. The division of some skins and a woman taken this morning. It is hard to divide one woman, Krell."

"Give her to the man who killed the most Hillpeople. Then the others will see the profit in bravery." He passed the musket to Apella. "Your next improvement. Notice what we've done to the striker. See how it holds the priming powder more securely? Fewer misfires." Pushing his chair back, Krell got to his feet. "When I return, we'll give you other improvements. A rifled barrel—a means to shoot farther and straighter."

"They must have a workshop," Kirk whispered. "Let's go...."

It was McCoy who spotted the shed. It was a ramshackle affair, set back from the street, but the black bulk heaped beside it was interesting. "Coal," McCoy said, "necessary for a forge. And those bags, they reek of sulphur, an ingredient of gunpowder. Thus, logically, my dear Captain, their workshop."

"Thank you, Mr. Spock." Kirk's face suddenly sobered. "Sorry. I know you're worrying about him, too."

"About that walking computer? Yes, I am."

The lock on the shed's door was as dilapidated as the building. Embers had been left to flicker in the still-open forge. Scattered around it were wooden gunstocks, bullet molds, iron rods to be bored into weapon barrels. McCoy's tricorder hummed over the ingots; but Kirk had moved to a barrel-boring device. He tested its point with a piece of iron. To his surprise it clicked sharply. He unscrewed it. "People's exhibit number one," he said. "A chrome-steel drill point."

McCoy looked up. "This pig iron is almost carbon-free. No village furnace produced this." His tricorder passed over a barrel rod. "People's exhibit number two. Cold rolled barrel rods, fashioned to *look* handmade." He turned. "My apologies, Jim. You were right about the Klingons."

"Make recorder and scanner tapes on everything."

"Pity we can't include a Klingon. That would about wrap it—" He stopped. Footsteps and voices were nearing the shed door. They scrambled for concealment behind a dusty pile of cinders.

Krell entered, followed by Apella. He hung the village lantern he carried high on a hook. Behind the protective cinders, Kirk motioned to McCoy. Understanding, McCoy unlimbered his tricorder; and as Apella broke into speech, recorded the words. "I thought my people would grow tired of killing. But you were right, Krell. They see it is easier than trading. And it has pleasures. I feel them myself. Like the hunt, but with richer rewards."

The Klingon had lifted a rifle from the work bench. "You'll be rich beyond your dreams one day, Apella. A governor in our Klingon Empire. Unimaginable delights—" He paused, hearing the tiny hum of McCoy's scanner. He turned to look around him—and Kirk grabbed at a wooden gunstock. He flung it hard at the lantern. Sparks showered as its light went out. In the dimness Kirk leaped at Krell but the Klingon pivoted, catching Kirk on the shoulder with the rifle. McCoy, rushing forward, used the "exhibit" barrel to drop Apella and whirled to help Kirk. But Krell had tripped over an iron rod. His rifle went off—and he shouted, "Guards! Intruders! The work shed, intrud—"

Kirk's fist got him straight on the chin. He fell—but already the *Enterprise* men could hear running footsteps, yells, alarm shots. They made for the door. An armed villager, gun aimed, stood in it. Kirk, diving for his legs, tumbled him over the sill. Behind him Apella was up again; and again McCoy smashed down with the "exhibit" gunbarrel. They raced for the open door. Then they veered, making for the shadow behind the heaped coal. Armed villagers, converging on the shed, pelted past them. They waited. Then they broke from their shelter and fled. When the first bullet whined past them, they had rejoined Tyree.

Spock was no longer motionless. He had begun to writhe, his face distorted—and the body-functions panel's readings fluctuated madly. When a groan burst from his laboring chest, Christine Chapel rushed to the wall intercom.

"Doctor M'Benga to Sickbay."

"Nurse . . . nurse . . ."

She flew to the bed. Spock's eyes were open, glaring wildly as he tried to control his twisting body. Twice he struggled again to speak and failed. The third time, his trembling lips succeeded in forming words. "Quickly . . . strike me. Pain will . . . help me . . . to consciousness. Strike me!"

Christine shrank back. "Hit you? No,—"

"Strike me!" He was gasping for air. "Unless . . . I return to . . . normal consciousness quickly . . . it will be . . . . too late. . . ."

She hit him.

"Harder . . ."

She slapped him harder. His breathing improved and his voice more certain. "Again! Then again. Pain . . . helps me back . . . to consciousness."

She struck him once more. As she hauled off for the fourth time, Sickbay's door snapped open. Scott stood in it, jaw dropped as she landed the blow on the bedridden Spock. He leaped across the room, grabbing her arm. *"What are you doing, woman?"*

M'Benga came through the open door. He strode to the bed, pushing Scott and Christine aside. Then he struck Spock with all his strength. He struck him again and again. The flabbergasted Scott was staring in horror. It was clear that the entire medical staff had gone out of its mind.

But Spock was sitting up. "Thank you, Doctor. That will be sufficient."

M'Benga spoke to Scott. "You can release her, Mr. Scott. She was only doing what she should have done." He gestured to the body-functions panel, whose needles were steadying into positions normal for Spock.

"A Vulcan form of self-healing, Engineer," Spock said.

He now astounded all but M'Benga by swinging his legs to the floor. As he made to stand, Christine moved an instinctive hand toward his arm. He congealed her with one of his arched-brow looks. "I am quite recovered, Nurse," he told her coolly.

She took the cool line herself. "Yes, I see you are, Mr. Spock."

The Doctor who had interned in a Vulcan ward herded everyone out of Sickbay. As the door snapped shut behind the three, Spock began knee bends.

Tyree was not an enthusiastic student of armaments. He listened courteously while Kirk explained the eccentricities of the flintlock taken from the guard the night before; but it was clear that connections between strikers, sparks and the ignitions of gunpowder failed to arouse the martial spirit in him. Kirk placed the gun against his shoulder. "Now aim it as I showed you," he said.

McCoy, emerging from the cave, frowned at what he saw. The gun fired obediently; but the bullet, kicking up dust near the skin target, ricochetted away.

Tyree dropped the gun. Kirk gave him a friendly pat on the shoulder. "Very good," he said. But he had seen McCoy's look. "Not here, Bones. We'll talk in the cave."

Tight-lipped and angry, McCoy followed him into the cave. Kirk had the look of a man who has considered all alternatives, arrived at an unpleasant decision and intends to back it up.

They hunkered down on the cave floor and McCoy burst out. "Do I have to say it? It's not bad enough there's already a serpent in this Eden of yours teaching some of these people about gunpowder. You're going to make sure they *all* know about it!"

Kirk's voice was quiet. "Exactly. Both sides must receive the same knowledge, the same type of firearms..."

"*Have you gone out of your mind?* Yes, maybe that's it. Tyree's wife. There was something in that root she used. She said that now you could refuse her nothing."

"Nonsense! Believe me, Bones, I've *agonized* over this, thought it through most carefully."

"Is it a coincidence that this is exactly what she wants? I wonder..."

"She wants *superior* weapons. And that's the very thing

neither side can have. Bones, listen. The normal development of this planet was status quo between the villagers and the Hillpeople. The Klingons changed that with the flintlocks. If this planet is to continue to develop as it should, we must equalize the two sides again—and *keep* them equal."

McCoy stared at Kirk in unbelief. "Jim—that condemns this whole planet to a war that may never end. You'll breed battle after battle, massacre after massacre. . . ."

Kirk slammed his fist on the ground. *"All right, Doctor!* I've heard . . ." He got up as though movement might somehow move him out of this ugliness. It didn't. But he'd got himself under control. He turned back. "Let's say I'm wrong. Even say the woman drugged me. So let's hear your sober, sensible solution to all this."

"We could collect all the firearms. Unfortunately, we can't collect the knowledge they've been given."

"No."

"Suppose we gave Tyree some weapon of overpowering force, something that would quickly frighten the villagers away." McCoy hesitated. "Trouble is, we've no guarantee what power of that kind might do even to Tyree."

Kirk waited. Finally he said, "Remember the twentieth century—the brush wars on the Asian continent? Two giant powers involved, much like the Klingons and ourselves. Neither felt they could pull out. . . ."

"I remember. It went on bloody year after bloody year."

"What would you have suggested, Bones? That one side arm *its* friends with an overpowering weapon? Mankind would never have lived to travel space if that had been done!" Kirk got up to pace the length of the cave. "We can't take this planet back to where it was! The only solution is what happened then—a balance of power. If it can be kept in balance long enough . . ."

"But if the Klingons give the villagers more power, what then, Jim?"

"We give this side exactly that much more. The trickiest, most difficult, dirtiest game of them all—but the only one that preserves both sides. In whatever this planet is to become, each side has its evolutionary value."

McCoy's face had grown deeply thoughtful. "Jim, all this time . . . with Tyree blindly trusting you—and you beginning to understand what you'd have to do . . ."

Kirk nodded. "Agony, Doctor. I've never had a more difficult decision."

McCoy looked at him, himself experiencing Kirk's torment. "There's another morsel of agony for you. As Tyree won't fight, he'll be one of the first to die."

"He'd be a wise leader," Kirk said. He stopped his pacing. "His wife's the only way to reach him. If I tell her we'll supply guns, she may persuade him. I must have a talk with her."

She was bathing in a forest pool. Cooled and refreshed, she finally stepped out of it, her wet inner garment clinging to her body. There was a flat rock near the pool and she sank down on it, zestfully savoring the sun's warmth as it began to dry her streaming black hair. After a moment she reached for her small leather pouch. Selecting a small herb from it, she crushed it between her hands, applying its scent to her neck, face and shoulders. She wore the concentrated look of a woman preparing herself for a man.

When she heard Kirk's voice call her name, she smiled to herself, unsurprised. Discarding the herb, she gave her attention to arranging her slim body advantageously.

At the sight of her in her thin wet clothing, Kirk hesitated. She beckoned to him. "Stay," she said. "You are here because I wished you here."

He smiled, correcting her. "I'm afraid this was *my* idea."

"Yes, they always believe they come of free will. Tyree thought the same when I cast my first spell on him." She touched the stone beside her invitingly. "Be comfortable, Kirk. Sit down. I will not hurt you."

After another moment of hesitation, he obeyed. She leaned toward him. "Can you smell the fragrance on me? Some find it pleasing."

He took a fast sniff at her shoulder. "Yes, very nice," he said. "But what I want . . . want to talk of . . ." The polite smile on his lips faded. His head was spinning.

Nona edged closer to him. He tried to draw back but his befuddled senses were stronger than his will.

"Smell the scent again," she said. "You will find it soothing."

"Yes, but I came to ... to talk about ... about...."

From where he had been following Kirk, Tyree heard the voices. He carried the flintlock whose mechanism still puzzled him. Now he forgot the question he had planned to ask. Face set, he checked the amount of powder in the pan. Then he moved on in the direction of the voices.

Nona had drawn Kirk close to the herb perfume on her neck. Kirk pulled away. Fighting vertigo, he got shakily to his feet, inhaling deep gulps of fresh air. "Forgive me ... I ... seem ... unable to think...."

She sat very still, smiling and waiting. Kirk's eyes locked with hers. And suddenly he was smiling back, aware only of a lovely woman who seemed to desire him.

"How beautiful!" he said. "How lovely you are, Nona!"

Tyree raised the gun. For a moment he focused its sights on Nona. Then he swung them slowly to Kirk. Nona, in Kirk's embrace, caught the gleam of sun on the barrel. She made no move though Kirk's back was Tyree's clear target. There came the sound of the weapon's crash on a rock. Relief mixed with contempt in her face. Tyree could never be important. A man of faint heart. She lifted her arms to Kirk's neck.

"Yes, lovely ... incredibly lovely," Kirk was saying foggily.

Tyree was running from the scene of his betrayal. As he skirted a rock, a monstrous shadow rose from behind it. The dead gumato's female mate, it had begun its swift and noiseless stalk of the Hillman when it was distracted by the sound of Kirk's maunderings. It swerved. Nona saw it over Kirk's shoulder. She tried to pull free but he held her tight. Fists clenched, she struck at him savagely, jerked clear of his arms and sped into a run. Then the sudden thought of Kirk's dazed helplessness halted her. Her quick stop brought a snarl from the beast. She screamed, racing for the pool. But the apelike thing cut her off at the water's edge. She shrieked again; and Kirk, slowly emerging from his confusion, fumbled for his phaser. Realization hit him. Rushing to the pool, he saw Nona prone, the great animal towering over her. He fired his phaser. The gumato vanished. Extending a hand, he helped Nona to her feet.

The assistance exhausted his strength. His drugged state had left him so weakened that he slumped to the ground, eyes closed, breathing hard. Nona looked down at him. Then she picked up a rock. She clubbed him over the head with it. The phaser dropped from his hand. She lifted it, examining it in wonder. Then she turned and made for the forest.

Stumbling, broken, Tyree was making his way to his lean-to when McCoy and Yutan intercepted him.

"Where's Captain Kirk?" McCoy demanded.

Tyree waved blindly behind him and Yutan cried, "Tyree! The firestick! Where is it?"

"I left it . . . back there."

"A fine thing to leave lying around! Show us!" McCoy shook Tyree's arm.

It roused him. "I show you," he said.

Pieces of the broken rifle lay on the ground. Yutan picked up the barrel. Tyree covered his face with his hands. "No! I don't want to see it!"

McCoy was about to speak when Kirk staggered toward them. Still groggy from the blow, he swayed. Then he crumpled back to the ground. McCoy, taking a quick check of his pulse, broke out the hypo from his medikit.

Meanwhile, Nona had arrived at a decision. At first sight of an armed village patrol, she had hidden herself behind a thick-leaved bush. As it approached, she made up her mind. She stepped from her concealment, confronting the leader of the four-man group. She lifted Kirk's phaser full into his view.

"I bring victory to Apella!" she said. "He will have the courage to use this new weapon! Take me to him!"

The man grinned. "Tyree's woman! A *Kahn-ut-tu* female also. Do we entrust this division to Apella?"

The patrolmen guffawed. The leader grabbed her, the others pressing around them. She yanked free. Then she aimed the phaser at the leader. "Touch me again—and this small box will kill you!"

The man hesitated. But the villager behind her gave her a slight push. She wheeled to level the weapon at him. He was not impressed. All of them were grinning broadly now. They closed in about her, clutching at her, at her clothing. Ignorant of how to use the phaser, she tried to shove them away. "Fools!" she cried. "I bring you a weapon far greater than your firesticks!" Laughing, one of the men pushed her at another one. She struck out, screaming. They began to toy with her. Their laughter had acquired a dangerous edge. One of them tried to kiss her. She shrieked again.

Kirk heard her. He reached for his phaser. "Nona! She's taken my phaser! She's in trouble! Come on...."

There was another scream. Her thin garment was ripped now. Passed roughly from jeering man to jeering man, she beat at their faces with the phaser, screaming wildly.

Kirk, McCoy and the two Hillmen raced down a hill toward her. The patrol leader, looking up, saw them. "Men," he yelled, "it's a trap! The woman tricked us!" His sharp knife gleamed. He struck.

"Nona!" Tyree shouted.

The leader lifted his flintlock, aimed and fired. McCoy fell.

Kirk, Tyree and Yutan charged the patrol. The fight was hand to hand, bloody and brief. The two surviving villagers fled. McCoy, holding his wounded arm, stumbled down to the scene of the melee. Tyree was stooped over the dead body of his wife. In the dirt, trampled but undamaged, lay the phaser. Kirk picked it up.

"She gave it to them," McCoy said. "But they didn't recognize it."

Kirk looked at the wounded arm. "You, too," he said.

"Yes, me too! You and your blasted Paradise planet!"

Tyree had straightened. He reached for an abandoned flintlock. Then he removed the powder and bullet pouch from a patrolman's dead body. He turned to Kirk, his grim face working with grief and fury. He extended the gun toward Kirk.

"I want more of these! Many more!"

"You'll have them," Kirk said.

Tyree spoke to Yutan. "Two of those who killed my

wife escaped. We shall track them down and kill them. Come! I must speak to our people."

They set off at a run. There was a moment's silence before McCoy said, "Well, you've got what you wanted."

"Not what I wanted, Bones. What had to be."

Amazingly, his communicator, so long silent, beeped. He flipped it open. "Kirk here."

"Spock, Captain. I trust all has gone well."

"Spock!" McCoy shouted. "Are you alive?"

"A ridiculous question, Doctor. Clearly you are hearing my voice."

McCoy shook his head. "I don't know why I was worried. You can't kill a computer."

Kirk motioned him to silence. "Spock, ask Scotty how long it will take to reproduce a hundred flintlocks."

Scott's voice spoke. "I didna get that precisely, sir. A hundred what?"

"A hundred . . . serpents, Scotty. Serpents for the Garden of Eden." He paused. "We're very tired, Mr. Spock. Beam us up back home."

THE OMEGA GLORY

(Gene Roddenberry)

The disease which had killed every crew member aboard the USS *Exeter* was a mystery. Everything about the other starship was mysterious. Why was it still patrolling an orbit around the planet Omega IV when it was scheduled to end its mission six months ago? The patrol was the current assignment of the USS *Enterprise*. That was the enigma which had caused Kirk to decide to transport his landing party aboard the *Exeter*.

And what he had been expecting was an undamaged starship full of dead men. If that had been an accurate description of the situation he'd walked into, Kirk would have been grateful. Dead men were a tragic but natural phenomenon. But there was nothing natural about the *Exeter*. That was the horror. The ship wasn't full of dead men. It was full of empty uniforms.

Phaser still in hand, he watched McCoy stooping over a collapsed uniform in the *Exeter*'s engineering section. A scattering of white crystals extended from its neck and sleeves. McCoy, waving him and Spock away, bent closer over the uniform, taking care not to touch it.

Lieutenant Raintree rushed up to him, his face sick. "Just the uniforms . . . all over the ship, Captain! And that . . . white stuff spilling out of them!"

Spock said, "As if they'd been in them when. . . ." His words trailed off into silence.

"Exactly," Kirk said. "When *what?*" He spoke to McCoy. "Bones, let's get to the bridge. Mr. Spock can replay the Captain's last log entry. They may have had time to record whatever was happening to them."

A blue crew uniform was crumpled on the deck beside the computer station. Spock stepped over it to turn on the mechanism. McCoy, his tricorder unslung, was examining the tiny white granules at the end of its sleeves. He lifted his head. "Jim, analysis says these crystals are thirty-five percent potassium, carbon eighteen percent, phosphorus 1.0 and calcium 1.5."

"I have the surgeon's report, Captain," Spock said. "It seems to be the log's last—"

McCoy interrupted. "Jim! The crew hasn't left! They're still here!" At the look on Kirk's face, he went on. "This white powder . . . it's what's left of the human body when you remove the water from it. We're all ninety-eight percent water. Take it away, and we're just three or four pounds of chemicals. Something crystallized the chemicals in these people. It reduced them to *this*."

"So that's it," Kirk said slowly. "At least we can hope it was painless."

The computer beeped. Activating a switch, Spock pointed to the main viewing screen. "The name of the *Exeter*'s surgeon, sir, was Carter," he said.

The face of a man appeared on the screen—the face of a man in torture. So much for the hope that the deaths had been painless, Kirk thought. That agonized face had possessed a body. He visualized the body dragging itself to the recorder to speak its last words into the Captain's log.

They began in mid-sentence. ". . . if you've come aboard this ship, you are dead men." The voice broke in a spasm of pain. "Don't return to your own ship. A mutated di-bacto-viro complex of some sort . . . deadly . . . don't know what it is. If you're aboard you're infected— you're already dying."

Young Lieutenant Raintree whispered, "My God—let me out of here!"

"Pull yourself together, Lieutenant!" Kirk snapped. "This is heroism you're listening to!"

"Repeat, repeat," said the face on the screen. "Our landing party brought . . . contamination up from the planet." The face convulsed with agony. "You have one chance . . . some kind of immunity for those living on the planet's surface. Your sole chance, get down there. *Get down there fast.* The Captain is. . . ."

A scream broke from the viewer. It went dark.

After a moment Kirk walked over to the vacant command chair. Carter had sat in it to use the Captain's log recorder. Now all it held was the bodiless clothing that had been his medical officer's uniform. As to the heap of white dust dropped from the clothing—that was Carter.

"Bones," he said quietly, "warn the *Enterprise*. Mr. Spock, the *Exeter*'s Transporter Room. Prepare to beam us all down to the planet."

They were in an alley of what might have been an old-time American frontier settlement, set on the edge of a desertlike terrain. But the buildings that formed the alley's walls were Asian, their roofs concave, flaring at the eaves. They moved cautiously to the alley's entrance. In the street people had gathered about some object of intense interest. They looked Asian, too. Dark-haired, yellow-skinned, their eyes were slanted by the epicanthic fold characteristic of Oriental races. One of the villagers saw them as they emerged from the alley. He gave a terrified shout. The others turned—and the crowd broke up into a frightened flight.

The object of their interest was an execution. A headsman's block had been set up in the middle of the street. Kneeling at it, his hands thonged behind his back, was a savage-looking white man, his strongly-muscled body clad in skins. Near him stood a young white woman, also wearing savage skins. Horrified, Kirk realized she was awaiting her turn at the block. Instinctively, he and his men rushed forward. The villagers who were holding the white male savage were surprised into loosening him. He rolled aside as the ax flashed down. He tried to sink his teeth into the nearest villager. The ax was lifting again when it was halted by a sharp command.

"Put your ax away, Liyang!"

The voice was familiar. Kirk whirled.

Incredibly, Captain Ronald Tracy of the USS *Exeter* was striding toward him in the well-known uniform of a starship Captain. His pistol-phaser hung at his belt. Nor had he lost the commanding charisma of the personality Kirk remembered. He was followed by a military guard of young village men armed with javelins and swords.

"Ron!" Kirk shouted.

"Jim Kirk, by all that's holy!" Tracy said.

There was an odd little pause in which Kirk was conscious that Tracy was taking stock of the unexpected situation. Then he seemed to have straightened out the inventory. "I knew someone would come looking for us," Tracy said. "I'm sorry it had to be you, Jim." He shook hands grimly. "But I'm glad your arrival stopped this. I didn't know they had an execution going on."

Kirk said, "Captain Tracy. My First Officer, Mr. Spock; ship's surgeon Leonard McCoy; Lieutenant Phil Raintree."

McCoy said, "Captain Tracy, the last log records aboard your vessel warned of a mutated disease."

"You're all safe," Tracy said. "Some form of immunity exists on the surface here." He turned to a robust guard behind him. "No more of this, Wu. Lock up the savage."

Wu pointed to Kirk's phaser. "They carry fireboxes—"

"Lock up the savage!" Tracy said.

It took more than Tracy's military guard group to subdue the still-bound white man. Before he was led away, several villagers had to be told to assist them. It was a rough assistance. Tracy noted Spock's cocked eyebrow. "The white beasts are called Yangs," he said casually. "Impossible to even communicate with them. Hordes of them out there; they'll attack anything that moves."

"Interesting," Spock said. "The villagers know what phasers are."

Tracy glanced at him sharply. "You're a Vulcan?"

Spock nodded. "By one-half, Captain."

Was Tracy disturbed by the information? Kirk broke the moment of curious tension. "How were you left alone down here? What happened?"

Tracy's answer came with obvious effort. "Our mediscanners showed the planet as perfectly safe. The villagers, the Kohms here, were friendly. That is, they were after they got over the shock of our white skins. We resemble the Yangs—the savages. When my landing party transported back to the ship, I stayed behind to arrange our planet survey with the village elders." He paused, struggling back to control. "The next thing I knew, the ship was calling me. Our landing party had carried an unknown disease back."

He stopped to avoid an open break in his voice.

"My crew, Jim. My whole crew . . . people I knew, people who. . . ."

He straightened his shoulders but couldn't go on. Kirk, sharing his torture, said, "We saw it, Ron."

"I . . . am as infected as they were . . . as *you* are. I stayed alive only because I stayed down here. There's some natural immunization that protects anyone here on the planet's surface. I don't know what it is yet."

McCoy spoke to Kirk. "Lucky we found that log report. If we had returned to the *Enterprise* . . ."

Tracy completed the sentence. ". . . you'd be dying by now along with the whole *Enterprise* crew. You'll stay alive only so long as you stay here. None of us can ever leave this planet."

They had half-suspected it—but hearing it finally put into words chilled them. Being marooned on Omega IV for the rest of their lives could well be a fate as empty as death. Kirk, aware of his men's somber faces, said, "Then we'll have to make the best we can of this planet. Can this place provide us with any quarters?"

"They're being prepared," Tracy said. "Wu will show Doctor McCoy and the Lieutenant to theirs. Doctor, yours can accommodate any equipment you want beamed down to you. I apologize, Jim. Your quarters and Mr. Spock's aren't ready. So if you two will follow me . . ."

He led them to a building that clearly served the more prosperous villagers as a kind of clubhouse. Its large central room featured a charcoal brazier. Richly dressed men sat at tables eating strips of meat broiled over the brazier. As Tracy entered with his guests, the villagers respectfully moved from their tables to clear a path for them. Two elders hurriedly relinquished the brazier table. At the sight of Kirk, one of the attractive girls who were busy setting the table with fresh dishes dropped a cup.

Tracy beckoned her back. "They were afraid of me, too, at first," he said. "It's our white skins; our likeness to the Yangs, the white savages."

He might have been a feudal thane graciously permitting his serfs to sit themselves below the salt in his superior company. No acknowledgement was made of his fellow-diners' nods or spoken greetings. His ease with their excessive deference made Kirk more uncomfortable than the deference. He accepted food from one of the girls; and deliberately ignoring Spock, said to Kirk, "Barbecued wild game. Sort of a long-necked rabbit-antelope."

A meat slice was speared and extended to Kirk. Holding it, he watched another girl rush to fill their crude cups with drink.

"You are treated with a considerable honor by these villagers, Captain," Spock said.

Again, he was ignored. Pointedly, Tracy addressed himself to Kirk. "These Kohm villagers asked for help, Jim. If they ever had any spirit, it's been whipped out of them by the savages."

"Are all the Kohm villages under attack?" Kirk said.

Tracy nodded. "This is one of the last. But before the Yangs began decimating them, they appear to have had quite an advanced civilization. There are ruins of large cities out there."

Spock had taken all the snubs he intended to take. Just as pointedly as Tracy, he ignored the *Exeter*'s Captain to speak directly to Kirk. "Though nomad tribes have been known to destroy advanced civilizations, they rarely trouble an unarmed people—spiritless villagers."

Tracy sprang to his feet, furious. "I will not be questioned by a subordinate!"

Unperturbed, Spock merely eyed him curiously. Kirk's voice had become formal. "Captain Tracy," he said, "I think you're forgetting that Mr. Spock is my First Officer. He holds the rank of Commander in the service."

Spock rose to his feet. "I see no purpose in my causing anger to Captain Tracy," he said politely. "May I remove myself, Captain Kirk?"

Kirk took a sip of his drink. Then he nodded. Spock quickly left the table. As he disappeared, Kirk turned a cold face to Tracy. "Let's clear something up right now, Captain. I have never had a better 'First' than Mr. Spock—or a better personal friend."

"You're sentimental, Jim. I've yet to meet a Vulcan capable of friendship. Certainly this one is doing his best to sabotage ours."

Tracy's ruddy face had grown accusing. "And you know what's in his computer mind, too! It's added up a few scanty observations—and clicked to the conclusion I've violated the Prime Directive! He's got it into his machine head I'm interfering in this culture!"

Kirk said to himself, *Take this easy*. To Tracy he said, "Ron, a First Officer's job *is* to be suspicious." He put a smile on his face. "Saves his Captain from appearing to be the villain."

"I am a fellow starship Captain," Tracy said.

"Fair enough. So you are. Yet I myself saw the local militia recognize our phasers. They also seem to take orders from you." He hesitated. "I'm not making any charges, believe me. I'm merely asking what goes on."

Tracy's eyes searched Kirk's. "All right. So long as we're asking questions, I'll put one to you. Suppose you were faced with a horde of incredibly vicious savages you knew were massing for a final attack—one that would erase the last trace of a planet's civilization. And suppose there were enough phasers to repel the attack? Can you imagine the power made available to this Kohm culture by just five phasers?"

"Sure," Kirk said. "Like introduction of the atom bomb into the crossbow era."

Tracy leaned forward intensely. "Jim . . . within forty-eight hours the Yangs would slaughter every adult and child in this village."

Kirk found the intensity disturbing. He spoke very quietly. "Ron, every time man interferes with the natural evolvement of another world, he ultimately destroys more than he saves."

"When they attack, Jim, where do *we* go? There's no place left! You and I are finished, too!"

Kirk said, " 'I solemnly pledge I will abide by these regulations even in death.' " He gave the gravity of the words a long moment before he added, "That is the oath we both took."

Tracy leaned back in his seat, stretching. "So you'll try to stop me."

"I won't 'try,' Ron. I will stop you."

The sole way to enter McCoy's quarters was to sidle in. The village room he'd been assigned was jammed with medical research instruments beamed down to him from the *Enterprise*. Privately, Kirk wondered if the ship's lab had left itself enough equipment to make a simple blood test. Now, as he wriggled over to the electron microscope, McCoy looked up from the slide he'd been studying.

"Our tissue definitely shows a massive infection, Jim. But something down here *is* immunizing us. Otherwise, we'd have been dead ducks hours ago." He removed the slide, frowning at it. "Problem: it could be anything. Some spore, some immunizing pollen, some chemical in the air. Just finding it could take months, even years."

"Bones, we may not have much time to isolate it."

"I've got only one lead. The infection resembles a virus used during Earth's bacteriological war of the 1990s. Hard to believe the human race was once dumb enough to play with such dangerous bugs."

Spock spoke from the door. "A Yang lance, Doctor. It got the Lieutenant under the shoulder." The Vulcan, his uniform begrimed, was supporting the wounded Raintree, pale with loss of the blood that darkened his uniform's shoulder.

"That mat over there," McCoy said, grabbing his medikit. Raintree was groaning with pain as they settled him on the mat. Kirk eyed Spock. "You all right?"

"Just bruised, sir. We were approximately a hundred meters out of the village when five of the savages ambushed us." Kirk glanced quickly at the phaser hanging from his belt. Noting the look, Spock said, "I subdued them with the neck pinch, Captain. Our phasers were not used."

"Good," Kirk said. "Mr. Spock, do you see any hope that these Yangs can be reasoned with? A peace parley, a truce until. . . ."

Raintree struggled to lift his head from the mat. "No, Captain . . . they're too wild, practically insane."

Nodding, Spock said, "Captain Tracy seems to have established several facts. One—the Yangs' total contempt for death makes for an incredible viciousness. Two—his statement that the Yangs are massing for attack is valid. There are signs of thousands of them in the foothills beyond." He paused to remove two objects from under his shirt. Laying them on the lab bench, he said, "However, in one important matter, Captain Tracy is less truthful."

"Phaser power units," Kirk said slowly.

"Yes, sir. Captain Tracy's reserve belt packs. Empty. Left among the remains of several hundred Yang bodies. A smaller attack on this village occurred a week ago. It was repelled by Captain Tracy with his phaser. I've found villagers who corroborate this fact."

Kirk, his face hard, replaced the empty phaser pack on the bench. McCoy looked up from the wound he was swabbing. "Jim . . . he'd lost his ship, his crew. Then he finds himself the sole bulwark between savages and the massacre of an entire village of a pleasant, peaceful people. . . ."

Spock said, "Regulations are harsh, Doctor—but they are also quite clear about any violation of the Prime Directive."

"Without a serum we're all trapped here in this village," McCoy said. "Under these circumstances the question of arresting the man is a purely academic one."

"I agree that formal charges have little meaning now," Spock said. "My suggestion is that Captain Kirk confiscate his weapon."

"Yes," Kirk said. "And file a report." He reached for his communicator. "Starfleet should be made aware that—"

"It is I who will send the messages, Jim."

Tracy stood in the doorway, his phaser leveled at them. On his mat Raintree made a move toward his belt. Tracy fired the phaser at him. Its beam struck him full in the chest, enveloping him.

Kirk lunged. The deadly phaser swung to point directly at his heart. He halted. Then he just stood, frozen with shock. The Captain of a starship . . . a phaser . . . and a wounded member of the service. He didn't turn to look at the charred mat which had once held Lieutenant Raintree.

Tracy's militia was efficient. Despite the spears they used to round up the *Enterprise* trio, they first saw to it that phasers and communicators were removed. As Wu placed them at Tracy's feet, the *Exeter* Captain opened his own communicator.

"*Enterprise,* come in," he said. "This is Captain Tracy of the *Exeter.*"

The satisfaction on Tracy's face told Kirk that Uhura had answered him. Sulu, taking his temporary command very seriously, would be standing beside her at her console.

"I'm afraid I've got some bad news for you," Tracy was telling Uhura. "Your Captain and landing party beamed down too late for full immunization. They've been found unconscious. I'm doing everything I can for them."

Kirk waited, hot rage building up in him. Tracy, smiling at him over the communicator, said, "There'd be no point to risking the lives of additional medical staff, Mr. Sulu. This is a fatal disease. They are courageous to volunteer to beam down. However, as I have acquired some immunity, your people may pull through, too. Meanwhile—"

Kirk had torn free. "*Sulu!*" he shouted. "*Don't let—*"

The butt of Wu's sword crashed down on his head. Dark flooded in over him. Spock had pivoted fast. But Wu was just as fast. He'd placed his sword's point on the unconscious Kirk's throat.

Tracy snapped off the communicator. He pointed to Spock and McCoy. "If those two open their mouths, Wu, kill them."

Tracy's communicator beeped. He flicked it open, listening. "Sorry, Mr. Sulu. All members of your landing party are running high fevers. Captain Kirk is delirious. Nobody is in any condition to speak to you. The villagers are helping me to make them as comfortable as we can."

But the strange Captain's words failed to satisfy an agitated Sulu. Tracy's communicator beeped again. He opened it with irritation. But there was no trace of it in the bland voice that said, "Mr. Sulu, let's have an end to this. *I am trying to save the life of your Captain.* What you heard was not the start of an order to you. It was the cry of a man in delirium. Speak to your medical staff. They will tell you that delirious people shout because they are suffering. I am doing my best to reduce your

Captain's. I will keep you informed of his state on condition you permit me to attend to it. Tracy out."

The vague shadow in the doorway gradually assumed the shape of one of Tracy's militiamen. Kirk discovered that he could see again. McCoy's makeshift lab. His arms hurt. They were bound. He sat up. The head at the doorway didn't turn. Then the hot rage surged through him again, galvanic. Head down, he charged the militiaman guard. He knocked him off balance and was preparing to charge again when Tracy pushed the guard aside with a terse "Leave us!"

Kirk sat down on the bench. In his own ears the scorn in his voice bit like acid. "Captain Ronald Tracy, per Starfleet Command regulation six, paragraph four. I merely mention it."

The smile he got was as false as the man. He'd hit home.

"I know," Tracy said. " 'You must now consider yourself under arrest unless in the presence of your most senior fellow officers, you give satisfactory answers to etcetera, etcetera, etcetera.' " He nodded. "Those are the first words duty requires you to say to me. Consider them said. You're covered. How about moving on to the next subject?"

"Which is 'why?' " Kirk said.

"Good. Direct, succinct." Moving some of McCoy's equipment aside, Tracy sat down on the lab table. "Answer: whatever it is that's immunizing us now has protected the inhabitants of this place against all sickness. And for thousands of generations. Soon your doctor is going to discover what mine did. *No native of this planet has ever experienced any kind of disease.* How long would a man live with all disease erased, Jim?"

"He might stay young a hundred years, live to be two hundred maybe."

Tracy went to the door, calling. Wu came in. "Tell Captain Kirk your age," Tracy said.

"I have seen forty-two years of the red bird. But my eldest brother—"

Tracy broke in. "Their year of the red bird comes every eleven years. Wu has seen it forty-two times. You can multiply. Wu is four hundred and sixty-two years old. Or more, since the year here is longer. His father is well over a thousand. Interested, Jim?"

"It's not impossible, I suppose," Kirk said.

"I said . . . *are you interested?*"

"Of course I'm interested! I expect McCoy could verify all this easily enough."

"He will if you order it! We must have a doctor researching this!" He leaned forward with that special intensity characteristic of him. "Are you grasping *all* this immunizing agent here implies? Once it's located, it is a *fountain of youth!* Virtual immortality!"

"For sale by . . . ?"

Kirk waited for Tracy's nod. He got it.

"For sale by those who own the serum," Tracy said. "McCoy will eventually isolate it. Meanwhile, we inform your ship you're still sick. Order it away. When we're ready, we'll bargain for a whole fleet to pick us up if we want it. They'll send it."

"Yes, I guess they would," Kirk said.

"In the meantime, we've got to stay alive. Let the Yangs destroy what we've got to offer by killing us—and we've committed a crime against all humanity! I'd say that's slightly more important than the Prime Directive, wouldn't you?"

Kirk had gotten one arm free of his bonds. He came to his feet fast; and was yanking the other one loose when he saw Wu stiffen.

"*Tra—cee!*" The militiaman shouted.

Cool, easy, self-assured, Tracy rose from the table. Kirk's right arm was held by the thong just an instant too long. Tracy's expert swing cracked against his jaw, sending him stumbling to his knees. He jerked his right arm clear of the noose. Tracy pulled back for a feinted swing; and Kirk, dodging, exposed his jaw to a judo chop that spun him around. He recovered, lashed out with his right fist— and Tracy, moving with the blow, chopped him again, slamming him to the floor.

"Not bad, Jim," he said. "Considering I'm larger, faster, more experienced than you are, it wasn't bad at all." He yanked Kirk to his feet. "In better shape, too, I fancy. Physical fitness has always been one of my—"

Kirk pivoted, lunging for his chin. Tracy ducked. He lifted his hard hand for another chop. Once more he smashed Kirk to the floor.

This time he didn't pull him to his feet. Instead, he strode to the door to call Wu and two militiamen. Pointing to Kirk, he said, "Bring him!"

They took him to the village jail.

There was a rack of swords in its outer room. That was all Kirk had time to register before he was dragged to the inner area. The cells were fitted, not with bars, but with elaborate grills. The first one held the two Yangs who had escaped execution. The powerful male appeared to be anything but grateful. Snarling with rage, he'd thrust an arm through the grillwork, trying to reach the yellow-skinned militiaman who stood guard at the next cell, which confined Spock and McCoy.

Tracy, his own phaser leveled at Kirk, handed the three *Enterprise* weapons to Wu. "Give these to your men. Tell them we leave soon. This time we'll ambush the Yangs with many fireboxes." He pointed to McCoy. "Have the Doctor taken back to his work place. The one with the pointed ears stays."

McCoy made a protesting move; and Kirk said, "Go ahead, Bones, continue your research."

As McCoy left with Wu, Tracy jerked a thumb toward the Yangs' cell. "And you, Jim, take a close look at that."

The male's eyes were a blue blaze of fury. Yet, taking that good look at him, Kirk discerned a certain stoicism underlying the ferocity—a kind of native dignity that suggested the man was a person of consequence in his tribe. As to the young woman, there was a supple grace even in the way she leaned back against the cell wall, her eyes alert under her shock of unkempt blond hair.

"*Animals* which happen to look like us," Tracy said. "You still believe the Prime Directive's for this planet, Jim?"

Kirk said, "We lack the wisdom to interfere in how this planet is evolving."

Tracy wheeled to his men. "Put him in there! If logic won't work, maybe that will!" They hesitated, incredulous. "Put him in there!" Tracy shouted.

Fearfully they opened the cell door. The Yangs rushed at them. Beating them back with sword and spear butts, two militiamen hastily shoved Kirk inside, slamming shut the heavy iron grating. It was locked and the keys replaced in a table drawer. Kirk faced around to see that the Yangs had begun to circle him like wolves stalking fresh meat.

He addressed the male. "If you understand me—"

A foot smashed against his shin. He tripped—and the Yang was on him, hands at his throat. Instead of fighting the choking fingers, he twisted suddenly; and doubling his legs up, lashed out in a hard kick that caught the man in the midriff. But the blow won him only a moment's respite. The Yang used his crash against the wall to roll into a crouch and begin the stalking again.

Tracy, turning to leave, called, "Remember that Prime Directive, Jim!"

The circling went on as though both Yangs drew on inexhaustible springs of energy. The female, seeing an opening, leaped on Kirk's back; and he had to turn to slam her away, pivoting just in time to fight off the male. Then once more the stalking began.

In his own cell, Spock, pressed against the grilled door, was straining to see into Kirk's. "Don't they ever rest, Spock?" Kirk yelled. His uniform shirt was ripped. And he was becoming aware of diminishing strength. There'd been that black-out from Wu's sword-butt crash on the head. Tracy's judo chops hadn't been so salubrious, either. Now here was the strain of a constant vigilance as these tireless Yangs watched for an off-guard moment. Just five seconds rest . . . He spoke to the Yang. "At least tell me *why* you want to kill me!"

Spock called, "Keep trying to reason with them, Captain. It is completely illogical that they—"

"I am very aware that this is illogical, Mr. Spock!"

The Yang jumped him again. The struggle sent the woman flying against the door's iron lattice. Spock reached an arm out to give her his Vulcan neck pinch. The male paused in amazement as she collapsed. He went to her, trying to shake her awake. Disturbed by his failure, he leaned against the door to peer into Spock's cell.

THE OMEGA GLORY

The Vulcan was at its window, pulling at its ornate grillwork. Watching, the savage saw him heave his full weight against the iron embedded in the ancient mortar. A thin trickle of crumbled dust fell on the sill. Spock called to Kirk. "I think I've loosened my window grill a bit. If the mortar on yours is as old . . ."

"I can't even test it. Not with them on me every moment."

But the Yang had held off. Kirk eyed him. The woman sprawled at his feet was slowly reviving. Once conscious again, would she incite her mate to resume the stalk? "Keep talking, Spock. Don't let me doze off."

"Captain Tracy mentioned there apparently was a considerable civilization here at one time. A war is the most likely explanation of its ruin, Captain. Nuclear destruction or a bacteriological holocaust."

"An interesting theory," Kirk said. "Better keep working on your window, Spock, if we're ever to regain our freedom."

In the very act of renewed attack, the Yang male froze. "Free-dohm?" he said. He was staring at Kirk with mixed curiosity and awe. "Free-dohm," he repeated.

"Spock!"

"I heard, Captain. Ask him if he knows what it means."

"That is a worship word—*Yang* worship!" cried the savage. *"You will not speak it!"*

Kirk said, "It is *our* worship word, too. Perhaps we are brothers."

"You live with the Kohms!"

"Am I not a prisoner of the Kohms now, like yourself?"

He let it rest there. Moving to the cell window, he began to tug at its grillwork. It was immovable. He flung a shoulder against it—and was rewarded with a small sifting of powdered mortar. The Yang looked at his mate. She rose to her feet, lithe as ever, and they both came over to join him. All three pushed their combined weight at the lattice. More mortar fell; and Kirk, turning to the Yang, said, "Why did you not speak until now?"

"You spoke to Kohms. They are for killing only."

The listening Spock called, "Is your window giving, sir?"

"A little . . . we'll get yours next."

Their following heave broke the grill loose at one corner. Now they had leverage. Twisting and bending the iron, they released its top. The old mortar finally surrendered. It was the Yang who wrenched it free. Smiling, Kirk turned his head toward Spock's cell, calling, "Stand by, Mr. Spock. We'll have you out in—"

"Captain!" Spock yelled.

The warning came too late. The heavy grill had caught Kirk on the temple, felling him, unconscious, to the floor.

The Yang shoved his mate through the open window. Spock saw him hoist himself up to the sill, and disappear.

"Captain?"

Spock, crouched at his cell door, tried to reach the unmoving body of Kirk. But it had fallen under the open window at the other side of the cell.

The recovery of consciousness came slower this time. Finally, hearing Kirk move, Spock left his cell window to hurry to its door.

"Captain?"

"Spock? How long?"

"About seven hours, sir."

Seven hours out . . . a rest of sorts. Blood had dried on Kirk's face. Trying to move, he winced at the tide of pain that washed over him. The iron lattice lay beside him. He used its support to get groggily to his feet. Over his head the open window gaped. Stumbling, he put the grill at a slant under the window. Then he climbed it, hauling himself the shortened distance up to the sill. In the alley outside, he located the jail's rear door. It opened; and he hurried to the table drawer where the cells' keys had been placed.

It was Spock who discovered that Tracy had placed a guard in McCoy's quarters. The man stiffened at the scratching noise that came from the door. McCoy, oblivious to everything but his portable computer, didn't so much as look up. When the scratching came again, the guard carefully opened the door. He literally stuck his neck out for Spock's Vulcan pinch. He folded, dropping his sword. Spock had him dragged inside the room before McCoy looked up to register a world beyond his computer.

"Oh . . . Jim," he said. "Good morning."

Spock, eyeing the lab equipment, saw an instrument that might lend itself to conversion into a communications signaler.

"I can cross-circuit this unit, Captain. We can contact the *Enterprise* in a few moments."

"Bones," Kirk said, "what have you found?"

"I'm convinced now that there was once a frightful biological war. The virus still exists. The crew of the *Exeter* was killed by it; we contracted it, too. But over the years nature has built up immunizing agents in the food, water, soil. . . ."

Spock, busy with tools, observed, "The war created an imbalance: nature counterbalanced."

McCoy nodded. "These natural immunizers just need time to work. That's the real tragedy. If the *Exeter* landing party had stayed here just a few hours longer, they never would have died."

Taking in the statement's implications, Kirk said, "Then we can leave any time we want to?"

McCoy nodded again. Kirk's face lightened with his first grin in a long time. Then it disappeared. "Tracy," he said, "is convinced this immunizing agent could become a fountain of youth. Isolate it, make a serum, inject it into others."

"Poppycock!" McCoy snorted.

"Bones, some of them here live to be a thousand years old."

"Possible. Because their ancestors who survived had to have superior resistance. And they developed powerful protective antibodies in their blood during the wars. You want to destroy a whole world, maybe your descendants can develop a longer life—but I hardly think it's worth it."

"Then any serum you develop out of this is useless."

McCoy shrugged. "Who knows? It might finally cure the common cold. But lengthen our lives? I can do more for you if you'd eat right and exercise regularly."

Over at the corner bench where he'd been working on the lab instrument, Spock made some final adjustment; and looked up to say, "Somewhat crude, Captain, but I can signal the ship with this. No voice contact possible, of course."

"That will be quite sufficient, Mr. Spock." Kirk was moving toward the bench when the signaler in Spock's hand glowed red under the brilliant beam of a phaser. It disappeared—and Spock was slammed violently backward, grazed by the fierce energy in the scorching beam.

Tracy, his uniform spattered with blood, was leaning against the doorframe, disheveled, wild-eyed. He lowered the phaser. "No messages," he said. He glanced around the room. "Kirk, the Yang in the cell with you. Did you set him free?"

Kirk ignored him to join McCoy, who was kneeling beside the wounded Spock. "Alive at least," McCoy said briefly.

"The savage, Kirk! Did you send him to warn the tribes?

Kirk looking up, saw that Tracy was badly shaken. "What happened?" he said. "Where are your men?"

"The Yangs must have been warned. They sacrificed hundreds just to draw out into the open. Then they came . . . and came . . . and came." His voice trembled. *"We drained three of our four phasers and they still came! We killed thousands and they still came!"*

Tracy became suddenly aware that he was shouting. He made a visible effort to control himself, and McCoy, intent on Spock, said, "He'll live. But I'll have to get him to better facilities than these."

"Impossible," Tracy said. "You can't carry the disease back up to your ship."

"He's fully immunized now," McCoy told him. "All of us are!"

"We can beam up any time, Tracy," Kirk said. "Any of us."

"You've isolated the serum?"

"There *is* no serum!" Kirk said. "There are no miracles here—no immortality! All this has been for *nothing!*

Tracy stared at him, dumbfounded. Then, unbelieving, he looked at McCoy. "Explain to me, Doctor! *Explain!*"

"Leave medicine to medical men, Captain!" McCoy snapped. "You've found no fountain of youth! They live longer here because it is now natural for them to live longer!"

Color drained from Tracy's face. Even the cuts on it had gone pale. He raised his phaser, motioning Kirk to the door with it. "Outside," he said. "Or I'll burn down both your friends now."

He'd do it, too, Kirk knew. "Do what you can for him, Bones," he said and walked to the door.

The frightened villagers had left the street empty.

Tracy, phaser pointed at Kirk, tossed him a communicator. "Let's see how willing you are to die," he said. "Call your ship!"

Silent, Kirk looked at the communicator. "I need your help, Kirk!" Tracy cried. "They'll attack the village now! My phaser is almost drained; we need more, fresh ones."

So that was it. The *Enterprise* was to get into the weapon-smuggling business to accommodate this madman. At the look on Kirk's face, Tracy shouted, *"You're not just going to stand there and let them kill you, are you? If I put a weapon in your hand, you'll fight, won't you?*

Reason, sanity. Was Tracy any longer capable of either one? Kirk said, "We can beam back up to the ship. All of us."

"I want five phasers . . . no, make it ten. Three extra power packs each."

"All right," Kirk said. The phaser lifted and aimed at him as Tracy waited. Kirk clicked the communicator open.

"Enterprise, this is Captain Kirk."

He could hear the relief in Uhura's voice. "Captain! Are you all right now?"

"Quite all right, Lieutenant. I want ten phasers beamed down, three extra power packs each. Do you have that?"

Uhura didn't answer. "Say again!" Tracy said.

"Enterprise, do you read?"

Sulu's voice spoke. "This is Sulu, Captain. We read you—but surely you know that can't be done without verification."

"Not even if we're in danger, Mr. Sulu?"

A good man, Sulu. And smart. "Captain, we have volunteers standing by to beam down. What is your situation?"

Tracy made an impatient gesture.

"It's not an immediate danger, Mr. Sulu. Stand by on the volunteers. We'll let you know. Landing party out."

Kirk snapped off the communicator. Tracy nodded in a begrudged approval. "You have a well trained bridge crew. My compliments." He extended his hand for the communicator. It was the chance Kirk had been waiting for. He grabbed the hand, twisted it; and lashing out with his fist, knocked Tracy off balance, reaching for the phaser. But Tracy eluded the reach and, rolling with the blow, came back with the weapon at the ready. As Kirk dived around a building corner, he fired it. The beam struck a rainbarrel—and the chase began.

The dash around the building corner put Kirk in an alley he recognized. It was the one that passed the jail's cellblock. Racing by a Kohm cart, he made for the jail. Behind him, Tracy leaned against the cart, kneeling to aim at Kirk's back. But his weight was too heavy for the flimsy cart. Its rear wheel collapsed. Kirk ran on. He jumped into cover through the jail's rear door. He was barely inside when a phaser beam blasted a porch support. He heard the porch crash down.

The iron lattice that had felled him—it would still be in his cell. He found it. Not much use against a phaser, but it was all he had. Opposite the jail's front door was the execution block. As he emerged from the door he saw Tracy standing beside it. The phaser came up. Tracy fired it point blank. Nothing happened. Tracy stared at the drained phaser. Then, flinging it aside, he grabbed up the executioner's ax. He charged Kirk, taking a murderous swing at him. Kirk ducked and slammed the iron lattice into his middle. Tracy fell, but kicking out, tripped Kirk; and the two closed, grappling in the dirt.

Tracy had kneed him in the groin when he gave a cry.

The point of a spear had pricked his shoulder. Both men looked up. The Yang stood over them. Behind him were ranged other armed white savages.

The brazier had been removed from the central table in the villagers' clubhouse. Now it held a worn parchment document, some ancient-looking books and Tracy's communicator. The whole interior of the room had been altered into what Kirk could only consider to be a primitive court scene. White savages composed the "jury." Among the men Kirk saw the young woman from the jail cell. He, Spock, McCoy and Tracy had been seated to the left of the table.

The male Yang of the jail cell strode to the seat behind the table.

He looked at Kirk. "My name," he said, "is Cloud William." Then he looked away to nod at one of his warriors guarding the door. A procession of Kohm Elders were herded into the room and up to the table. Kirk looked anxiously at the stiff figure of Spock. "I am weak, Captain, but not in difficulty."

McCoy leaned over to Kirk. "He *must* have attention, Jim! And soon."

Spock indicated the Kohms. "Prisoners, Captain. It seems they like killing less than we thought."

Kirk glanced around at the rough courtlike arrangements. "If my ancestors had been forced from their cities into deserts, the hills . . ."

"Yes, Captain," Spock said. "They would have learned to wear animal skins, adopted stoic mannerisms, devised the bow and the lance."

"Living much like Indians . . . and finally even looking like the American Indians." He paused, startled by his own sudden idea. "Spock! Yangs . . . yanks . . . Yankees! Is it possible?"

Spock nodded. "Kohms . . . kohmunists. Almost too close a parallel, Captain. It would mean they fought the war you avoided and here the Asiatics won, took over the Western world."

"And yet if that were true, Spock, all these generations of Yanks fighting to win back their land . . ."

"You're a romantic, Jim," McCoy said.

He sat back in his chair. Yang warriors were pushing their Kohm prisoners into attitudes of respect. The crash of a drumbeat's ceremonial tattoo silenced the room. Proud and tall, Cloud William rose from his seat behind the table.

"That which is ours is ours again! It will never be taken from us again." He pointed to the rear door and a steady drumbeat throbbed. *"For this day we mark with the great Ay Pledgili Holy!"*

Turning to look, Kirk, Spock and McCoy stiffened in unbelieving amazement. The door had opened. A guard—an honor guard—had entered. One carried a staff. From it hung an incredibly old and tattered flag, its red, white and blue faded by time. But its stars and its stripes had outlasted the centuries' ravages. They had triumphed over time.

Kirk, watching the flag proudly planted in its stand at the front of the room, felt his blood chill with awe.

Tracy whispered, "The American flag!"

Kirk turned to Spock. "After so long, I wonder if they really understand what they were fighting for."

"I doubt it, Captain. Some customs remain, but most of them would have become only traditions by now."

"And ritual," McCoy said. "The flag was called a 'holy.'"

Tracy said, "They can be handled, Kirk. Together, it will be easy." He leaned toward the three of them. "I caution you, gentlemen, don't fight me here. I'll win—or at worst, I'll drag you down with—"

He was silenced by a nudge from a spear. Cloud William was speaking. "I, Cloud William, am chief, also the son of chief, Guardian of the holies, Speaker of holy words, leader of warriors. Many have died; but this is the last of the Kohm places. What is ours is ours again."

The words were repeated by the crowd. "What is ours is ours again!"

Cloud William placed his right hand over his heart. "You will say these holy words after me." The Yang guards placed the Kohm prisoners' right hands over their hearts. Cloud William turned to the old flag. "You will all say Ay pledgli ianectu flaggen tupep likfor stahn . . ."

Kirk sprang to his feet. ". . . and to the republic for

which it stands. One nation, under God, indivisible, with liberty and justice for all!"

The room exploded in shouts. A guard, moving to Kirk, halted in shock.

Cloud William was in quiet but agitated conversation with an aged savage at his table. The old man, shaking his head, referred to one of the yellowed books on it. Guards were removing the Kohm prisoners from the room. Two warriors, uneasy and uncertain, moved toward Kirk. One motioned him to face the Yang chief.

The chief was rapping the butt of his knife on the table to quiet the room.

"You know many of our high-worship words. How?"

Kirk said, "In my land we have a—a *tribe* like you."

"Where is your tribe?"

Kirk pointed upward. "We come from there. From one of those points of light you see at night."

Uproar broke out again. Kirk tried to go on but his words were drowned by the noise. Cloud William rapped for quiet once more. He turned to nod at the old Yang scholar beside him. The still-keen eyes fixed on Kirk. "Why are you here? Were you cast out?"

The Yang jury waited for his answer. Kirk spoke carefully. "You are confusing the stars with 'heaven' from which—"

"He was cast out!" Tracy shouted.

He jumped from his chair to confront the jury. "Don't you recognize the Evil One? Who else would trick you with your own sacred words? Let your God strike me dead if I lie!" He looked upward. "But He won't because I speak for Him!"

The brutal murder of Raintree . . . the betrayal of his service oath . . . now this exploitation of ignorance and superstition. He should have known, Kirk thought. To further his purpose there was nothing that Tracy would not do. But the old Yang scholar had hurriedly opened a thick, black book.

Cloud William was studying Tracy. "Yet you have killed many Yangs," he said.

"To punish them. You would not listen when I tried to speak with you. *You* tried to kill *me*."

Kirk said, "I am a man like yourself. I am not God. I am not the Evil One."

"Would a *man* know your holy words?" cried Tracy. "Could a *man* use them to trick you?" He extended a dramatic finger at Spock. 'And see his servant! His face, his ears, his eyes! Do Yang legends describe the Evil One?"

Kirk turned to the tribunal. "Do all *your* faces look alike? Can you tell from them which of you is good and which is bad?"

The old scholar had pushed the black book before the chief. Cloud William lifted it to kiss it reverently before he opened it. Kirk saw that its worn gold-lettered title was still legible. It read "Holy Bible." A wrinkled hand extended a finger to point to a page.

Many old Bibles contained illustrations. If this one pictured drawings of Lucifer's aides, one of them might bear some resemblance to Spock. One apparently did. Cloud William looked at Spock. Then he looked back at Kirk.

"You command the demon," Tracy said to Kirk. "Everyone has seen it." He wheeled to the chief. "You want more proof? The demon has no heart! Put your ear to him!"

Guards had seized Spock. The chief left the table.

McCoy cried, "His heart is different! The Vulcan internal organs are—"

"I have seen his sorcery," said Cloud William. He fingered the back of his neck. "When he touched my woman there, she fell into sleep." He crossed to Spock and solemnly placed his ear against the Science Officer's chest. Listening, a frown began to gather on his forehead. He straightened up. "He has no heart."

The room burst into terrified yells. They subsided as Cloud William raised his right arm. Then he hurried back to his ancient mentor. "There is a way," he was told. Painfully, the aged scholar moved to a large ornate box at the end of the table. Cloud William nodded in obvious relief.

"The greatest of holies," he said. "Chiefs and the sons of chiefs may speak the words . . . but the tongue of the Evil One would surely turn to fire." He looked straight at Kirk and Tracy. "I will begin and you will finish." He closed his eyes, chanting, "Ee'd pebnista nordor formor fektunun . . ."

His lids lifted. He waited.

There was something unplaceable but familiar in the chanted words. As Kirk struggled to identify them, Tracy cried out, "He fears to speak them for indeed his tongue would burn with fire! Kill his servant unless he speaks, so we may see if the words burn him!"

A Yang knife was poised at Spock's abdomen. The clamor for blood turned the room into bedlam. Cloud William, his face deeply troubled, had given the signal for the knife plunge when Kirk shouted, "No! Wait! There's a better way! Your sacred book, does it not promise good is stronger than evil?"

"Captain . . ." But over Spock's protest rang out the voice of the young Yang woman of the jail cell. "Yes, it is so written! Good will always destroy evil!"

"It is written," said the old scholar.

The guards had bound both Kirk and Tracy. Now a Yang warrior cut their thongs. The room had been cleared of furniture. In its central space Cloud William drove two razor-sharp knives into the floorboards. Kirk tried to rub circulation back into his numbed hands.

"Careful, Jim," McCoy said. "I've found Evil usually triumphs unless Good is very, very careful."

Kirk nodded wordlessly. He walked over to where the two knives thrust upward from the flooring.

"The fight is done when one is dead," Cloud William said. Lifting his arm, he dropped it swiftly, shouting, "Hola!"

Tracy was the first to reach his knife. He shoulder-butted Kirk aside and kicked his knife away. Then he lunged, knife raised. Kirk met him and, seizing his wrist, immobilized the down-thrust. They locked in a wrestle, straining against each other for an opening.

McCoy muttered, "We've got to do something, Spock."

Spock strove with his bound hands. "I am open to suggestions, Doctor."

Kirk broke free. He got a hammerlock on Tracy; but the *Exeter* Captain, wriggling himself out of it, was carried away by the momentum of his own move. Kirk stooped and scooped up his knife. The two began a wary circling of each other.

Spock suddenly became conscious of eyes. They belonged to Cloud William's young woman. He saw a tremor pass over her as their eyes locked. Half-fascinated, half-repelled, she tore her gaze from his. Then she looked at him again. He beckoned her toward him with his head. McCoy saw the gesture. "What are you doing?" he said.

"Making suggestions," Spock said.

Tracy had nicked Kirk. As he withdrew his knife, Kirk drove at him with a swift thrust; but Tracy parried the slash and the young woman, unnoticed, began to make her way through the shouting warriors. Edging along the wall, she reached the table that still held the old documents, the books and the communicator. She paused, glancing back at the two fighting men. Tracy's knife flashed out, cutting Kirk's sleeve and arm. Blood dripped to the floor. But the young woman had the communicator. Holding it so that it couldn't be seen, she moved toward Spock and McCoy. Spock looked up at her. "Do as my mind instructs you, woman," he said.

"I obey," she said.

Kirk was losing the fight. His shoulder was slashed now and the crowd howled for more blood. Then Tracy finally made his mistake. Caught off guard by a feint from Kirk, he stumbled. Kirk hauled back—and landed a blow that spun Tracy around and down. Kirk was on him, his knife at his throat. He held it there, his left hand reaching for Tracy's weapon. He wrenched it from him and sent it skidding across the floor to Cloud William's feet. A sudden silence fell over the room.

"Kill him," Cloud William said. "It is written Good must destroy Evil."

Kirk lifted the knife from Tracy's throat, rose to his feet and was backing away when he heard a familiar hum in the stillness. He whirled. Sulu and two Security guards had sparkled into shape beside him. Around the room Yang warriors were dropping to their knees. At stiff attention Sulu said, "Sir, we picked up a communicator signal but we couldn't raise anyone. Adding that to—"

THE OMEGA GLORY

"We'll discuss it later, Lieutenant. Put Captain Tracy under arrest. Now, Cloud William..."

The Yang chief had crawled to his feet. "You are a great God'servant, and we shall be your slaves."

Kirk reached down, lifting him to his feet. "Get up! Stand and face me."

"When you would not say the words of the holy Ee'd Pebnista, I doubted you."

Kirk said, "I did not recognize the words because you say them badly... without meaning."

The old Yang scholar had lifted the ornate box high in the air. Kirk approached him and gently removed it. He opened it, took out a ragged fragment of ancient parchment. Aghast, the old man cried, "Only the eyes of a chief may see the Ee'd Pebnista!"

"This was not written for chiefs." Kirk turned. "Hear this, Cloud William. This is *your* world. But perhaps without violating *our* laws, we can teach you what your fathers meant by these words."

He raised the tattered parchment so that all could see it. "Among my people, we carry many such words as this, from many lands, from many worlds. Many are equally good and well respected. But wherever we have gone, there are no words which have ever said this thing of importance in quite this way. Look at these three words written larger than all the others and with a special pride never written before or since... in tall words, proudly saying..." He paused.

"We the people..."

He faced Cloud William. "What you call the Ee'd Pebnista was not for chiefs or kings or warriors or the rich and powerful... but for all people. Over the centuries you have slurred the meaning out of the words. They are these...."

Reading from the parchment, he spoke slowly and clearly. "*We... the... people...* of the United States... in order to form a more perfect union, to establish justice, insure domestic tranquility, provide for the common defense, promote the general welfare, and secure the blessings of liberty to ourselves and our posterity—do ordain and establish this Constitution."

He reverently restored the parchment to the box. "Those words," he said, "and the words that follow were not meant only for Yangs. They were for Kohms also."

"For Kohms?" repeated Cloud William, shocked.

"They must apply to everyone—or they mean nothing. Do you understand?"

"I do not fully understand, one named Kirk. But the Holy words will be obeyed. I swear it."

Kirk left him to address Sulu. "You and your men will have to stay a few days until your bodies pick up immunization and adjust."

Sulu grinned. "Looks like an interesting place, Captain. You don't suppose there's a Shanghai or Tokyo down here, too?"

"There might be at that," Kirk told him. He clicked open the communicator Spock handed him. "Kirk to *Enterprise,* four to Transport."

"We're locking in on you, Captain," Uhura said.

Kirk, Spock and McCoy, Tracy between them, moved together for upbeam.

As they broke into dazzle, Kirk turned for a last look at the old flag upright in its standard, its stars and its stripes still bright.

ABOUT THE AUTHOR

JAMES BLISH, author of Bantam's popular *Star Trek* series, once won the coveted Hugo Award for his novel, *A Case of Conscience*. He has written many other Science Fiction novels and short stories as well. Mr. Blish, who is trained as a biologist and was formerly employed by several large pharmaceutical companies, is an American citizen presently making his home near Oxford, England. He was one of three persons who jointly founded the famous Milford Science Fiction Writers' Conference in the early 1950's, and, under the name of William Atheling, has written some of the most informed criticism of Science Fiction.

FREE!
Bantam Book Catalog

It lists over a thousand money-saving bestsellers originally priced from $3.75 to $15.00—bestsellers that are yours now for as little as 50¢ to $2.95!

The catalog gives you a great opportunity to build your own private library at huge savings!

So don't delay any longer—send for your catalog TODAY! It's absolutely FREE!

Just send us a post card with the information below or use this handy coupon:

BANTAM BOOKS, INC.
Dept. FC, 414 East Golf Road, Des Plaines, Ill. 60016

Mr./Mrs./Miss_____
(please print)
Address_____
City_____ State_____ Zip_____

Do you know someone who enjoys books? Just give us their names and addresses and we'll send them a FREE CATALOG too!

Mr./Mrs./Miss_____
Address_____
City_____ State_____ Zip_____

Mr./Mrs./Miss_____
Address_____
City_____ State_____ Zip_____

FC—6/74